The
DEVIL'S
CLAIM

The DEVIL'S CLAIM

USA TODAY BESTSELLING AUTHOR
GEMMA JAMES

ISBN-13: 978-1534845398
ISBN-10: 1534845399

This book is a work of fiction. Names, characters, and incidents are either products of the author's imagination or are used fictitiously. Any resemblance to actual events or persons, living or dead, is entirely coincidental.

Note To Readers

The Devil's Claim is a dark romance with a BDSM edge that does NOT conform to safe, sane, and consensual practices. Includes explicit content and subject matter that may offend some readers. Intended for mature audiences. Book two in the *Devil's Kiss* series.

1. INFERNO

He's waiting.

Waiting for me.

I could barely breathe in the small space of my bathroom. I gripped the sink, fingers curling around cold porcelain, and willed my galloping heartbeat to slow. He was going to hurt me. Physically, emotionally, psychologically. I knew this, yet it wouldn't change a thing. I would still unlock the door. Still pull it open and go to him…still give him my body.

"What the hell are you doing?" I asked my reflection. "Why are you letting him back into your life?"

The panicked woman in the mirror didn't have an answer.

I turned on the faucet in the tub and then removed my clothes, and for a few moments I concentrated on the roar of the water even though it did nothing to silence the alarm going off in my head. I hadn't been with a man in a year; a very long and lonely year, especially after experiencing how earth-shattering sex with him was. He'd given me a taste of something I hadn't realized I needed.

Like a dope dealer dangling a sample enough times until he had me coming back for more, begging on my hands and knees and selling my self-worth and my soul.

A soft knock startled me. "Kayla? Is everything okay?"

I warily glanced at the door, as if he could bypass the lock and come inside. He was good at bypassing things—my protests, my will, even the damn law.

"I'm fine." My voice broke, giving away my shattered state of mind. "I'll be out in a few."

"I'll be in the bedroom. Don't make me wait long."

My body broke out in goose bumps, and I couldn't decide if they were the good or bad kind. I sank into the hot water, closed my eyes, and let myself remember. The first time he'd slid his fingers inside me, he'd had me strung up on my toes, gagged and thighs spread wide. I'd been helpless and terrified. That fear still lived in me, but so did the undeniable longing to be taken by him again. I throbbed all over just thinking about his hands on me.

Fear and arousal—why those two visceral reactions went hand in hand for me, I didn't know. I might never know.

I finished bathing, and twenty minutes later, I stood in front of the door, my hand trembling on the knob. The comforting scent of coconut wafted from my warm, naked skin. Skin he'd left bruises and welts on a year ago.

This was a bad idea. Seriously, in the history of bad ideas, I'd win the award.

Here goes nothing.

The darkness of the hallway swallowed me, and I blinked my vision into focus as I padded to the bedroom. He'd turned off all the lights; now only the soft glow of the nightlight I left on for Eve illuminated the way. Thinking about her twisted my insides. My daughter's presence was the only thing that would stop me now, but I'd sent her away with Stacey for the night.

I'd left myself with no way out.

The door to my bedroom stood wide open, like a gaping hole waiting to suck me inside. Or maybe it was the man waiting in there, reeling me in with his gravitational pull. My heart thudded with each step, and I couldn't deny the dampness collecting at the juncture of my sex. He hadn't even touched me yet, but just the knowledge of him waiting, of what he could do to me—what he would do to me—made me tense with equal amounts of dread and anticipation.

I stepped into the bedroom, and his body brushed mine. He stood behind me, radiating heat and arousal; the air was so thick with it, I smelled it, tasted it. His hands drifted down my arms, his fingers curling around my wrists like shackles. He pulled them behind my back and secured them with something soft and silky.

"Gage?" His name came out a shaky sigh, escaping my trembling lips and no doubt making him rock hard. I was scared. I couldn't help it, couldn't hide it, despite knowing how he thrived on my fear—how he'd *always* thrived on my fear. The pain he'd inflicted a year ago came rushing back, and I couldn't catch my breath. A year was a long time, but not long enough to make me forget.

"I can't do this," I whispered, struggling to speak each word.

"Quiet." He spoke the command in a soft and gentle tone, yet the steel behind that single word ensured I pressed my lips together. "I'm going to make you come long and hard tonight, so long as you don't fight me."

"You know I can't," I choked, blinking back tears. "But I'm scared."

He fisted my hair, pulling until my neck became vulnerable to his mouth. His lips parted against my skin, and his tongue left a hot, wet trail down to my shoulder. The sensation was so arousing that my insides clenched from that single erotic kiss. I swayed into his body, feeling every hard plane of his nakedness, and shivered.

"I love your fear," he said, his confession rumbling along my shoulder. "But you don't have to be scared. Have you fucked anyone else?"

"No."

"Good."

His arms enfolded me and his palms shelved my breasts, thumbs and forefingers squeezing and twisting my nipples as he walked me further into the room. As soon as my thighs hit the mattress, he stepped away. I followed his progress around the bed, unashamed of blatantly ogling him. The soft light from the hall cast a glow on his skin, and I realized his body was just as firm as I remembered. If he hadn't tied my hands, I'd smooth them over his pecs, drifting lower until the muscles of his stomach quivered under my touch. Was he even capable of reacting like that? I couldn't recall; the past was a foggy recollection of pain intermingled with pleasure so hot it had branded me all those months ago.

He climbed onto the bed and stretched on his back. "Come straddle me."

Joining him became a challenge, considering he'd restrained my hands behind my back, but I managed to press one knee onto the mattress and hop up. His large hands reached for my hips, and my head spun as he settled me against the hard length of his cock. A simple adjustment, and he'd be inside me. A delicious shudder seized my body.

"Have you thought about me, Kayla? About this?"

Only every night. I blinked, refusing to give voice to the truth.

He dug his fingers into my hipbones. "Answer me."

My eyes drifted shut, and a small moan formed in my throat then broke free when he arched into me, just enough to tease. "Yes," I said with a groan. "I thought about you."

His hands glided up my sides and cupped my breasts. With a whimper, I leaned into his touch. "I thought of nothing else," he said. "A whole year thinking about you, of the way you smell…" He pulled my head down to his. "The way you taste." His mouth urged mine open, and his tongue swept inside for a mere second before he pushed me into a sitting position again. "It's not enough. I want to taste you all over."

I gasped when he hauled me up his body.

Oh God.

I lost my balance and almost hit the headboard, but

his hands braced me as he settled me over his face. I remembered the measure of his strength when he'd whipped me a year ago, and now he held me upright with that strength. My thighs shook as he licked between my folds. He found my nub and added enough pressure until I was bucking my hips and moaning his name, but each time release threatened to take me, he went back to teasing with the tip of his tongue.

"Please," I begged, panting, "let me come. It's been so long."

He groaned. "You're so fucking perfect. So wet." In one swift motion, he moved me down his body and entered me.

"Oh!" This was what I'd been missing—feeling him pulsing and alive inside me.

"Ride me until you come."

My hair curtained my cheeks in red waves, falling into my eyes as I rocked my hips, and I moaned with every slow slide. The sensation was both ecstasy and excruciating. He held onto my hips, never allowing me to fully sheath him, but I needed him deep.

"Please…"

"Who am I, Kayla?"

I groaned. "My Master." A loud cry poured from me. "Gage…deeper…"

He pushed higher. So incredibly deep. Oh God, he felt amazing—one hundred percent man, hard and slick and rubbing all the right places. Our bodies slapped together, damp with sweat and pure madness, and my name rumbled from his lips as he thrust to the hilt.

But it still wasn't enough, and he must have realized it too. The room spun, and I was on my back with him hovering over me. His breaths came hard and fast as he pressed me into the mattress, settled my ankles high onto his shoulders, and made our bodies one with abandon.

"So fucking good," he growled, burying his cock so deep a pang resonated in my heart. "You're mine. I'm never letting you go." He expelled a long sigh, and I drank him in, growing dizzy from the poison that was Gage. His mouth crushed mine, opening and plundering, tongue thrusting in time with our bodies.

My hands bit into my lower back, and my shoulders burned from being restrained, but the pain didn't register. Exquisite tension started in the arch of my feet, in the muscles of my legs, and crawled up my thighs until it pulled so tight at my core I was about to burst at the seams.

His mouth ate up my cries as the intensity pulled me under before launching me free. I came and came and came in a shuddering ball of surrender, soaring to a realm so high I was sure the crash would kill me, but damn if it wasn't a place I wanted to visit every night of my life.

Nothing had ever felt so wrong but so right, so painful yet unbelievably good, and nothing and no one existed in that moment except Gage Channing.

2. MINE

"God, you're gorgeous."

His whispered words woke me, though I didn't let him know I was awake. Early light crept beneath my lashes, and I listened to the morning song of birds, fearing he heard the drumming beat of my heart over the chirping melody.

His arms pulled me closer, flush against his chest, and he spooned me as if he didn't intend to let go. "I know you're awake."

"Pretend I'm not," I said, voice raspy from sleep. I wanted to pretend last night hadn't happened. Pretend I still had a modicum of sanity left. I'd built a life here for Eve and me, and I wasn't foolish enough to think that letting him back in wouldn't smash it to smithereens.

"I'm not good at pretending." His breath hitched, and for a few lengthy seconds, his silence pressed on me. "I need you. I need you so damn much it pisses me off. I'm crazy without you."

"You're just flat out crazy," I muttered.

His laughter vibrated against my shoulder. "I won't deny that statement."

The warmth and safety of his arms was an illusion, but I sank deeper into it anyway. "Where've you been for the past year, Gage?" Somewhere deep inside, I'd always known he'd come back for me…if he were capable.

He didn't answer right away. "Prison. I figured you knew."

"I…suspected." I'd seen the news reports about his arrest, but my own part in what went down haunted me, and I hadn't wanted to know what happened to him afterward. "What was it like in there?"

"It's not a place I'd ever send you." His arms tightened around me. "The worst part was being without you."

I stiffened. "What do you think is going to happen here?"

"You're coming home. That's what's going to happen."

"I am home. You can't just show up and start in on your demands. Things are a lot different from last year."

"Yes, they are. Fuck…I haven't felt like this since Liz."

His confession iced my veins. I untangled from his embrace and shot from bed. "No!" I cried, freaking out because he'd compared me to his dead girlfriend. The woman he'd loved—the woman he'd gone apeshit over. "Last night was—"

"Don't you dare say it was a mistake!"

I whirled at the sound of his rage, but it was too late.

He pinned me against the wall, hips smashing mine as his fingers bit into my shoulders. I couldn't breathe, and I sure as hell couldn't speak.

"I know what I am." He swallowed hard as his attention fell to my mouth. "I accept that I'm a twisted bastard, but I don't think you realize who you are."

My lungs finally worked, and I sucked in a breath. "Who am I?"

"Mine."

"You're delusional. I'm better off without you."

"No." He gave a determined shake of his head. "You're alive when you're with me. I recognize it in you. You need what I give you. Even the discipline and pain. Deny it all you want, but I know what I'm talking about." He brought his face closer, almost nose-to-nose. "You crave it. Tell me you haven't thought of me and gotten yourself off every fucking night for the past year."

I blinked rapidly, but hot drops of shame still coursed down my cheeks. "Why can't you just leave me alone?"

A trace smile flitted across his mouth, as if he knew I was incapable of turning him away on my own. I'd only be rid of him if he decided it. "You know why."

I shook my head, because I really didn't. I had no clue what he found so appealing about me. Why me? It was a question I'd asked myself constantly since this messed up arrangement with him first began.

His eyes smoldered as he loosened his grip on my shoulders. Two warm palms rose to cradle my cheeks, and I was still incapable of moving. "I'm in love with you."

"No," I moaned as more tears spilled over. "You

don't know what love is."

His fingers slid into my hair, tangling in the strands. He closed his eyes and brought his forehead to mine. "I'm selfish, controlling…cruel. Doesn't mean I don't know what love is." He brushed my lips with his. "I'm not in denial. What I did to you was fucked up. But Kayla?" His gaze found mine again, freezing me with the glint of resolve I saw there. "I'd do it again. I need you too much to let you go. I can be what you need, if you'll let me. I've had a year to find out what being without you is like, and I won't go another minute without you in my life, in my bed."

His mouth pressed against mine, and his kiss instantly possessed me.

Wrong. Bad. So bad. Tell him to leave and never come back.

"Gage?" I moaned into his mouth. I should have slept with someone else—maybe I wouldn't be so susceptible to his spell. "I hate you."

His mouth hovered, brushed mine again, and I felt the upward curve of his lips. The bastard was smiling. "Your head does." He settled a palm over my erratically beating heart. "But not here. And definitely"—he lowered his hand to the patch of hair between my legs—"not here. Here, you love me. You need me, so stop fighting it."

He forced my lips apart and dipped his tongue inside, but I wrenched my mouth from his. "It doesn't matter what I feel or don't feel. It's not important. I won't have you around Eve."

His eyes darkened to such a deep blue—the hue of

the sky after sunset but without the beauty of reds, pinks, and oranges to soften the emerging twilight. Just the darkness. Just Gage.

"I told you I'd never hurt Eve." His lips thinned, and his fingers shot out and held my chin in place. "*Never*, Kayla."

"But you'll hurt me, won't you?"

"I'll also make you scream my fucking name every night. I could tell you that by the time I'm done, you'll beg me to take you again, but that's a lie. I'll never be done with you."

Shaking my head, I tried to push him away, suddenly self-conscious of my nakedness, but he wouldn't allow it. "I can't do this with you. I can't go through this again."

"Things will be different. We'll discuss boundaries." He dropped his hands to his sides. "You say you can't? Well I can't be without you. There's no one else but *you*." It was the closest he'd ever come to begging, and the honesty in his voice pulled at me.

Damn him.

"How about I make us breakfast?" I asked. He stepped back, and I took the opportunity to slip by him. His appreciation burned along my skin as I dressed, and I didn't have to look at him to know he was watching my every move. But I glanced at him anyway and caught him reaching for his pants on the floor.

My blood rushed hot through my veins as he pulled the slacks up his legs, past the powerful build of his thighs, and I was certain my cheeks warmed to an obvious pink. How could someone so dark and rotten to the soul be so beautiful? The heat in his expression rooted me to the spot, and I swallowed nervously as he buckled his belt. That belt…I remembered that strap of leather all too well, and from the upturn of his mouth, he did too.

I breezed past him and left the bedroom. The worst he'd done since showing up on my doorstep yesterday was tie my hands behind my back, and his actions and words were almost gentle in the way he treated me now, but I wasn't about to fall into his trap. He'd show his true colors again eventually.

But did I want to be around when he did?

The sight of the kitchen stopped me cold. The space was tiny, the linoleum cracked in some spots and the counters faded with age, but the sink was clear of the dinner dishes I'd left the night before and the counters were spotless.

He leaned into me from behind. "I cleaned up last night while you had your freak-out moment in the bathroom." His arms looped my waist.

"Thank you," I mumbled, unsure of how to handle the varying emotions boiling inside me. Was this a trick? Why was he being so…*decent*?

"It was nice having a home cooked meal with you and Eve. Prison food leaves much to be desired." He released me and took a seat at my small dinette. "So what are you making me?"

I blinked before moving into action. The contents of my refrigerator made me cringe. I'd been so busy with work and Eve that I hadn't had time to go grocery shopping, but at least I had some eggs and cheese. "Omelets okay?"

"Yes."

I slammed the door shut, hating how off-balance his presence made me, and as I fixed our food, I allowed my mind to wander to a year ago. To the smack of his hand on my ass, to the force of his belt as it struck my skin.

The taste of his cock in my mouth as his hands held my head in place.

My breath grew shallow, from arousal, from fear. Gage was good at that—eliciting strong emotions that contrasted so sharply, they knocked a person on their ass in total confusion. I shouldn't want him. I should scream at him to get the hell out of my house and never come back. I should get a freaking restraining order.

As if the turmoil inside me didn't exist, I set our omelets on the table and calmly took a seat across from him. "What did you mean by boundaries?" I stabbed a bite and shoved it in my mouth. Raising my eyes to his turned out to be a mistake. His hypnotic stare paralyzed me; I couldn't look away if my life depended on it. I fell into the ocean of his gaze and almost missed the satisfied quirk of his lips. Almost.

"You know by now that a relationship with me won't be your standard variety. You'll have rules that govern your behavior."

"*My* behavior?"

"Yes. I expect you to obey me." He set his fork down and winced. "But last year I was cruel to you and that's not how I normally treat a woman. Not even when they beg me to hurt them beyond what I'm comfortable with."

"Then why?" I choked out. Everything he'd done hit me square in the chest, and his admission that he'd been exceptionally cruel hurt more than it should.

"I wanted to destroy what was his." He lowered his head with a frown. At least he had the grace to look ashamed.

"Congratulations." I let my fork drop, satisfied with the clatter it made. "You succeeded."

"No, I didn't. Your strength is both my frustration and my undoing. There's nothing more irritating or sexier on a woman." He took a bite, and his gaze veered up to mine. "And to clarify on what I mean by boundaries, we'll set limits this time. You'll have a safe word."

"You're talking as if we're going to be together."

"I'm not leaving here without you, Kayla."

His words crawled up my spine, and every inch of my skin broke out in goose bumps. Definitely the bad kind. Before I could form a thought, let alone a reply to that loaded statement, a knock sounded on my door, loud and insistent enough to be heard from the kitchen.

Stacey had taken Eve to preschool for me, and I'd called in sick the previous evening so I'd have time to deal with Gage's unexpected appearance. I had no idea who knocked at the door.

Gage scooted back, and his eyes narrowed to dangerous slits as he rose to his feet. "Expecting someone?" he asked.

"No." Shaking my head, I left the kitchen, knowing he was on my heels as I headed to the front door. My lungs deflated when I pulled it open.

This wasn't happening.

"Hi, Kayla." Ian's gaze swerved over my shoulder, and I didn't have to feel the warmth of Gage to know he stood inches behind me, most likely giving off a nasty territorial vibe.

A dark shadow passed over Ian's face, extinguishing the usual warmth of his expression. "I figured you'd be here," he told his brother.

3. LAST CHANCE

Had anyone been around to witness the spectacle in my living room, the three of us would have dropped jaws. I stood between Gage and Ian, my arms spread wide, a palm flat on each of their chests.

If they wanted to kill each other, they'd have to get through me first.

"This isn't happening here," I warned.

Ian withdrew first, his shoulders dropping in concession, but then his gaze veered to my disheveled hair and bare feet before swinging to take in Gage's naked torso. He spun me around so he shielded me from Gage.

"How could you be such an idiot, Kayla?" His verbal attack astonished me; it was so unlike Ian to lose his temper, especially with me. "A whole year, and you're still falling for his bullshit?"

"Is it really that shocking?" Gage asked. "She's still falling for yours after eight." He ripped Ian away from me, and his jealousy crowded the atmosphere in the room. "I bet there's plenty you've kept from her. Does she know about your infamous reputation, or does she still think you walk on water?"

Ian balled his hands, and my own began to shake. This wasn't going to end well.

"Shut your damn mouth. That was a long time ago."

"Not long enough," Gage said. "I certainly won't forget."

Ian shook his head. "Doesn't matter what I do or say. You won't budge."

Gage lurched forward, his face twisted in hatred. "You have no idea what you did that night!" He pushed Ian against the wall. "No fucking idea."

I settled my hand on Gage's shoulder, but my touch only made him flinch. "Gage," I said, keeping my voice low, but steady, "calm down."

He flung my hand off and stepped away. "I'll calm the fuck down as soon as he leaves."

Ian laughed, a bitter, spiteful rumble that chilled me. "You're crazier than I thought if you think I'll let you hurt her again. If anyone's leaving, it's you. I'll drag you out myself if I have to."

I'd never before seen this side of him. Ian was synonymous with gentle, loving, kind. Not hateful, though obviously, his brother brought out his temper. My foolish actions did too. I was hurting him, and I hated myself for it.

Make a choice, Kayla, and stick to it this time.

Three choices. One stupid beyond recognition, one safe and comfortable, and one so lonely the thought made me ache.

"You don't deserve her," Ian said.

Gage went rigid, and I sensed things were about to get even uglier. I planted myself between them again. "This needs to stop. I'm not a possession you can fight over." I almost rolled my eyes at the thought. There were so many women worthier of this shit than I was.

"As soon as he's gone," Ian said, stepping closer, "I'll convince you there was never a fight to begin with."

Gage snickered. The bastard actually snickered.

I shot a finger toward the front door. "Get out. *Both* of you," I said through gritted teeth.

Ian took a step back, uncertainty on his face, while Gage crossed his arms. His mouth turned up in a self-satisfied smirk. I wanted to hit him.

"I'm not going anywhere," he said. "We have things to discuss, or did you forget? I suppose we can forgo the boundaries, though I doubt you'll like that arrangement since you didn't take to it the first time around."

His cocky tone unraveled the last thread of my patience, and I shoved him toward the door. "Get out of my house!"

He stumbled backward, his sapphire eyes narrowing, and yanked the door open. "You're making a mistake. Trust me—you're not going to like the outcome."

I slammed the door in his face and stood stock-still for a few moments, listening to the clock on the wall tick away the seconds, keenly aware of Ian behind me. A fist pounded, making me yelp.

"I need my damn clothes!"

I stalked to the bedroom and gathered the last of his

things before throwing them onto the porch without a second glance. The door banged shut again, and I sensed Ian's gaze on me, though he didn't move. His presence only now caught up to me, and I fell into a state of shock, much like I had last night when Gage surprised me with his visit.

A whole year…

And I was still just as fucked up and confused as ever. A tear leaked down my face. I angrily brushed it away. "Why did you guys come here? I would have been okay."

Now he was moving, the softness of his flannel shirt rustling through the quiet as he neared me. I felt his heat, though he didn't touch me. "He got out of prison a few days ago, and I knew he'd come straight for you."

Which would explain why Ian had called more than usual this past week.

"I couldn't stand the thought of him hurting you again."

"He didn't." Not this time. This time, Gage had sent me soaring.

"I need to ask you something, and I want you to be honest with me."

I bit my lip.

"Are you in love with him?"

The space between us weighed heavily with silence, yet the roar in my head overshadowed it. In love with Gage Channing. Now wouldn't that be stupid? I gave him the only answer I could. "I don't know."

I was afraid to turn around and see how my words impacted him. Without warning, his arms came around me, and I tensed before sagging against him. His face nestled against my hair, nudging the strands aside and exposing my neck. His mouth caressed, open and hot and making me shiver until I melted. Ian still got me going and the realization came as such a relief.

"Did you sleep with him?"

A shameful sigh escaped my lips. "Don't make me answer that."

"You just did." The agony in his voice cut deep. He tightened his arms around me. "Give me one night, Kayla. If you can walk away from me afterward, then I'm gone for good."

"I don't deserve one night with you."

His protest vibrated against my collarbone. "Let *me* decide that. You need to stop blaming yourself."

He turned me around until we stood face to face, and his hands rose to frame my cheeks. "I want to show you what making love is really about because I think you've forgotten." His lips settled on mine and it was the briefest touch, the smallest of teases, yet achingly sweet all the same. "Let me love you."

"What if we do…and I still…let him come back?" I couldn't fathom it, had trouble saying the words even, but I didn't trust myself and I didn't want to hurt Ian anymore than I already had.

"Then I'll let you go."

"No," I said, shaking my head. "I can't do that to you."

"One night, Kayla. We'll go out and have a good time. No strings attached."

"There're always strings."

"You're right, but I'm cutting them now. Give me one chance to show you…"

My heart thumped at his words. "Show me what?"

"How much I still love you."

My mouth trembled, so I bit hard on my lower lip. Part of me wanted him.

Wanted to find out if I could still be normal.

But I feared the larger part of me that wanted Gage too much—the part that would hurt Ian because of the stronghold from which I couldn't break free.

"One night," he said again. "Besides, I think it's time we put all of our cards on the table. Gage is right—I have things I need to tell you, and I want you to hear it from me."

"Okay." The word was lost somewhere among the roaring in my head, and I knew I was making another mistake. Another wrong choice. Would I ever stop?

4. GIRL TALK

"Good God girl, what happened?" Stacey exclaimed as I ushered her and the kids inside. Eve didn't give me a chance to respond. Not that I would've known what to say anyway. She demanded my attention with her excited chatter about how "Aunt Stacey" took her out for ice cream.

"And we had movie night last night!" Her eyes rounded with childhood innocence, and she failed to notice the strained curve of my smile. Thank God she didn't question why mommy had been crying as I pulled her into my arms and held on tight.

Stacey's assessing gaze followed me into my living room. I set Eve down, and she took off running toward her bedroom with Stacey's son Michael not far behind her. Turning to face Stacey, I fisted my hand and held it to my mouth.

Don't start crying again.

I was normal here, known only as the quiet woman with the adorable daughter. I wasn't the criminal who allowed abusive men to take advantage—the messed up woman who got off on being controlled and punished.

"Gotta let it out eventually, Kayla. It's been festering for months."

I raised my eyes and blinked. "Wh…what?"

She took me by the elbow and led me to the couch. We sat side by side, and she rubbed my back in the soothing way my mother used to, long before she'd died. Long before the world's darkness had seeped into my veins and turned me into a shadow of myself.

"I know you've been runnin' from something. I figured you'd tell me when you were ready. Seems like you're ready now. So, who was the hottie in the shiny Benz last night?"

I wasn't sure how long we sat in silence, me chewing the inside of my cheek while Eve and Michael played in the next room. Stacey didn't push, didn't say a word. She was older, in her early forties and divorced. Michael had been her miraculous surprise late in life because she hadn't thought she'd ever get pregnant. She'd been quick to take me under her wing months ago. And as usual, she was right. I did need to talk about it but finding the words was another matter.

"His name's Gage Channing." I closed my eyes, rubbed my hands down my face, and little by little, what I'd done last night seeped in. "Oh my God."

"Let it out. You'll feel better."

"Last year, Eve was sick. She had leukemia." I glanced up and took in Stacey's stricken face. "She's okay now," I assured her. "I have Gage to thank for her survival. I was working as his personal assistant and one day...well, I stumbled on a way to steal the money I needed for her treatment, but he found out."

More silence. Eve darted from her room long enough to show me she'd dressed her doll by herself. "Wow," I said. "You are such a big girl!"

"Michael says dolls are stupid." She pouted.

"He's a boy, baby. Most boys think dolls are yucky. I bet he'll like your new puzzles though." She rewarded me with a toothy grin before returning to her bedroom.

"What'd he do when he realized you'd taken the money?" Stacey asked, bringing me back to our conversation.

A small laugh escaped, a bitter and crazy sound. "He blackmailed me into being his sex slave."

Stacey had no words, just wide and round eyes that assessed me in a different light. The whole story poured from me, and by the time I finished telling her everything, she'd gathered me into her arms. I muffled my cries so the kids wouldn't hear and gushed like a broken dam that wouldn't be stopped.

"I knew you carried a lot with you, but I had no idea, Kayla." She inched away to look at me. "Did he hurt you last night, or threaten you? Is that why you wanted me to take Eve out of here? We can call the police. He won't get away with this. Not while I'm around, honey."

I shook my head but couldn't meet her gaze. Shame warmed my cheeks, spreading until my body flushed. "He didn't hurt me. I...I..."

"You what?"

"I *wanted* him."

Her expression melted in pity, and I couldn't handle that look. I jumped to my feet, turned my back to her, and wrapped myself in my arms.

"It's classic, Kayla. He'll grovel and make you think he's sorry, promise not to hurt you again."

"Gage doesn't promise anything. That's what makes this so difficult. He is who he is and he doesn't hide or make excuses." Thanks to my ex-husband Rick, I'd become immune to those I'm-sorry-it'll-never-happen-again kind of tactics, but Gage was different. His hold on me was different, and I couldn't explain or categorize it.

Couldn't fight it.

"What does he want from you?" she asked.

"Me. He just wants me."

"What about Ian? Have you talked to him since all this happened last year?"

"He showed up this morning. He wants one night with me so he can…prove something, I guess." I rolled my eyes. "This is what most women fantasize about, right? Having two men fighting over them?" I collapsed onto the couch again. "I wish they'd never shown up. I was okay."

"No, you weren't."

My head snapped up at her matter-of-fact tone. "I was coping, Stace. I was *happy*."

"Coping? Maybe." She raised a perfectly shaped brow. "But you haven't been the picture of happiness, hon." She let out a heavy sigh. "So this is the reason you shoot down every man who shows any interest? This bizarre love triangle?"

"Trusting hasn't been easy. I don't have the best judgment when it comes to men."

"Your situation is far from normal, but for your own sanity you've gotta make a decision. Gage sounds like a monst—"

"He took a bullet for me." I paused, my throat constricting as tears threatened again. "He saved Eve. He's done *horrible* things, but…"

"Sounds like you've already made your decision."

I gave a rapid shake of my head. "No, Stace. No."

"If you didn't feel something for him, you wouldn't be sitting here so torn up. Some part of you must find him appealing, otherwise you wouldn't have called me last night to look after Eve." She grabbed my arm and my undivided attention. "You would've called the cops."

"I should've called the cops."

"But you didn't."

"It's just sex," I whispered.

She gave a sad smile. "It's never just sex, especially for someone like you."

I raised a brow. "Someone like me?"

"You believe in the fairytale—the happily ever after. I pegged you the minute you walked into Gigi's."

The corners of my mouth turned up. "Gage is *not* happily ever after. Ian is. He's what I need."

"But Gage is what you want."

"I don't know what I want. I thought I did, thought being away from both of them was the right thing to do."

"Maybe it is."

"I don't know anymore."

"Let me ask you this," Stacey began. "Which one would you trust with your daughter's life?"

When she put it like that…

"Both of them." But for entirely different reasons. One had used his money and power to save Eve, while the other would never hurt her, no matter what.

"Ian would make a great father," I said.

"Then maybe you should give him a chance. He isn't the one hurting you."

5. FAIRYTALE

Eve and I cuddled on the couch that night and watched *Beauty and the Beast* for what seemed like the hundredth time. It was her favorite Disney movie. It was also mine, which was why I'd introduced her to what I considered a classic. Now, having the perspective of a twenty-nine-year-old adult—and seeing the film through jaded eyes—I grudgingly realized why the movie had always appealed to me.

I was Beauty, and Gage was the Beast.

A submissive spirit had festered inside me for a long time; Gage had just brought it to the surface. But Stacey was right. I'd also dreamed of finding my Prince Charming since I was young, only I never imagined he'd come in the form of a true-life beast. Gage's ugliness stemmed from the core of his being, and unlike the beast of the fairytale, Gage was a master at disguise because you couldn't tell by looking at him.

Though once you glimpsed deeper, past the gorgeous face and sexy body, he was scary as shit.

"Why's he so mean to her? She's so pretty."

I swallowed hard, feeling as if Eve's question was somehow significant. "I think he probably hides a lot of pain, baby, and he takes it out on people he shouldn't."

Too true.

If Gage was the beast, then I didn't know how Ian fit into this twisted real life fairytale. He was much too likable to be Gaston. I sighed. I *should* give him a chance.

After the movie ended, I gave Eve a bath amongst a mountain of bubbles and giggles, and afterward, I took my time tucking her in tight, wrapping her up like a burrito. Her Cupid mouth relaxed as sleep pulled at her. I tiptoed toward the door.

"Mommy?" Her groggy voice halted me. "Can Gage eat here again?"

My heart pounded upon hearing his name fall from her lips. "I don't think so. Now go to sleep. I love you." I crept down the hall, my pulse accelerating as I neared my bedroom. Eve's questions haunted me. *Gage* haunted me.

His memory lived inside that room.

So did his scent; it surrounded me as I settled in bed, but I couldn't bring myself to strip the sheets yet. Hesitantly, I reached for my cell and dialed Ian's number five times before allowing the call to go through.

"Why do you want me?" I asked as soon as he answered.

Silence.

"Ian?"

"Give me a minute. I'm thinking, because if you're asking me that question, then you must be considering what I said, and I don't want to blow it."

I sank into the pillows and nestled the phone against my ear. "Okay."

A minute passed before he finally spoke. "When we got close in college, you touched a part of me no one had before. You saw me for who I wanted to be. Someone worthy. I want you forever. I want everything with you, and I would be honored to be a dad to Eve. I want to take your pain when you hurt, and I want to be the reason you laugh, even if you're laughing at me because I've said or done something ridiculously stupid." The line grew thick with silence, and I held my breath. "I come alive when I'm around you, Kayla. That's why I couldn't let go, even after all these years. No one comes close to you."

I knew how he felt, except the person who made me come alive was my childhood fantasy—a beast for sure.

"You're leaving me hanging here, Kayla." His breath shuddered over the line and into my ear.

"I know," I said quietly. And I couldn't do it anymore. I either had to let him all the way in, or let him go. "How long are you going to be in town?"

"I have a lot of vacation time saved up. I'm here for a while."

"You mentioned going out. When?"

"Anytime. Name the day."

"Are you sure?" I asked. "What if one night is all I can give you?"

"Then I'll take it. I'd rather give us one last shot than go my whole life regretting I never even tried."

I closed my eyes and attempted to block out the

bright depths of Gage's gaze, smoldering and lighting me on fire.

Get a grip, Kayla.

"How about tomorrow after my shift?" I knew Stacey would take Eve for me again, since she'd urged me to give Ian a chance.

"I'll be there."

The following evening came too soon. My room still haunted me, and I remembered Gage's hands on me in vivid detail. I got wet just remembering how his tongue lapped at me, how his body pressed me into the mattress and owned me. That night owned me. Gage had *always* owned me.

So why was I putting Ian through this? My heart refused to budge. It wanted what it wanted, and Ian wanted what he wanted; one more chance to make things right between us.

I finished dressing and quietly shut the bedroom door to the memories. He'd be here any minute and it wasn't fair to have Gage on my mind before our date even began. And wasn't that the only thing Ian had asked for? A final, fair chance? Letting him go would be the less selfish thing to do, but apparently, when it came to men, I wasn't the definition of selfless.

Ian made me hope. He made feel good about myself again. He wanted me so much he was willing to fight for me, even after a year. Even after the things I'd done.

His quiet knock unraveled me. I checked my hair in the hall mirror on my way to the living room, and my hands shook by the time I reached for the doorknob.

Dusk had fallen since I'd returned home from work, though the temperature was oddly warm. I was still accustomed to Oregon's cold and rainy weather in January. Ian stood on my doorstep, hands stuffed into the pockets of his blazer. His mouth curved into a brilliant smile, and God how that grin had the power to make me feel like the most important person on the planet.

I didn't deserve him. I knew this, yet I still allowed him to lead me to his rental car. It was nondescript, a white sedan to suit his needs while he was in town. Definitely not on the same playing field as the Mercedes Gage had shown up in a couple of days ago.

"You look...wow." He opened the door for me, and his eyes swept my body from head to toe. I wasn't wearing anything spectacular—just a lace cami and floral skirt that tickled my knees in the light breeze. A gauzy cover-up draped me, and my favorite part of the outfit was the white sandaled heels I wouldn't have gotten away with in Oregon this time of year.

"Thanks," I murmured with a smile. "You look good too, but you've gotta be hot in that." I gestured toward his jacket as I slid into the passenger seat.

"Not used to it being this warm." He removed his jacket, and the button down shirt he wore showed off his toned biceps. Instantly, a vision of him supporting his weight above me on those arms filled my head. I imagined his body sinking into mine, our foreheads coming together as our moans charged the air.

Maybe the problem wasn't the Texas temperature. Clearly, my hormones had taken me prisoner and had corrupted every facet of my being. Why else would I let Gage back in after all this time?

Oh God, don't go there. That's even worse.

"So where are we going?" I asked after he slid in behind the wheel.

His mouth quirked into a grin as he backed out of the driveway. "Into the city."

Butterflies took flight in my stomach. He was going all out.

What an understatement. We arrived at one of Dallas' more upscale restaurants. He ushered me inside, one hand resting at my lower back, and while he dealt with our reservation, I took a few moments to look around. Crisp, white linens covered strategically spaced tables small enough to offer the allure of intimacy, and a wall of trickling water sat tucked away in one corner. The hostess led us to a table near the waterfall, and the nervous flutters gained altitude once we were seated and left alone.

"So," he began, studying his hands. "I am curious about one thing."

I could only imagine. I braced myself, preparing for a difficult question I didn't want to answer. "And what is that?"

"How did you end up in Texas?"

I smiled, relieved. We'd had several conversations on the phone during the past year, mostly entailing of "how are you?" and "I miss you." He'd never asked how I managed to end up in such a small town so far from home.

"I got in the car and just started driving."

He raised a brow. "Seriously?"

"Seriously." I'd sold everything I owned to do it, though it hadn't been much. What hurt the most was letting go of my grandmother's locket my mom had passed down to me upon her death. "Never thought I'd make Texas my new home, but I stopped at Gigi's one morning for breakfast and that's when I met Stacey." She'd recognized a basket case when she saw one, and her kindness couldn't have come at a better time. I'd been on the brink of broke—in more ways than one—and tired of driving, but I'd been unwilling to return to Oregon.

"You continue to surprise me, Kayla." He dropped his gaze, and his expression melted in a frown.

"So," I said, my lips forming a smile despite the awkward silence. After a few moments, his did the same, though his grin came across as forced. Something told me he was thinking about his argument with Gage.

"I want you to know all of me," he said, "but once you hear the gory details of the person I used to be, I risk you walking away for good."

"It couldn't be any worse than what I've done." I lowered my head, and my hair obscured the shame flaming my cheeks.

"Kayla—" He began, but the waiter interrupted before he could continue.

With a formal smile that appeared plastered on the man's face, he presented the bottle of wine Ian had ordered and filled our glasses. "Ready to order, sir?"

Ian asked me what I wanted, which was refreshing after all the times I'd gone to dinner with Gage and he hadn't cared what I wanted. He rattled off our dinner orders and as soon as we were alone again, he cleared his throat.

"I was a little prick as a teenager," he said. "I slept around...a lot."

I glanced up, wondering where he was going with this.

"Liz and I were screwing around for months before Gage found out." He dropped his head, letting out a breath. "I drank constantly, did drugs at parties. I was a mess, but my dad refused to see it. He treated Gage like shit, but me...he put me on a pedestal. I was gonna be the college football star, maybe even go all the way to the NFL. As long as I kept my grades up enough to play, kept showing up at practices and performing well, he turned a blind eye to the rest."

"Why are you telling me this? What does your past have to do with the three of us now?"

"I wanted you to hear about it from me, not him. I'm far from perfect, so the next time you say you don't deserve me, I'm gonna lose it, Kayla."

I fiddled with the deep blue linen housing my set of flatware and wondered why even a freaking napkin made me think of Gage's eyes. "Thanks for telling me, but the past is just that. It was a long time ago."

"To Gage, it's not." He leaned forward. "I won't sugarcoat this, Kayla. What happened that night was my fault, and he has every right to hate me. I'm the reason Liz is dead."

"Why do I feel a 'but' coming on?"

"But that doesn't give him the right to hurt you to get

back at me." He reached across the table and enfolded my hand in his. "My dad abused him growing up." He swallowed hard. "I'm pretty sure he abused my mom too, but I was younger than Gage, and she protected me from it the best she could. Gage wasn't so lucky. When Liz died…I think it sent him over the edge. He's never been the same since, so don't kid yourself into believing you can change him."

"You changed," I pointed out.

He dragged a hand through his short brown hair. "How deep are you with him?" His question rattled me. Terrified me.

"I don't know what you mean."

"Bullshit. We're being honest here, remember? How deep?"

I locked my gaze on his. "When he comes around, I can't breathe, can't think, and for the life of me"—my voice splintered, and I looked away, unable to face him —"I can't say no to him. I don't *want* to say no to him."

"So it's sex then?"

"That's what I keep telling myself," I muttered.

"Jesus, Kayla. He's not gonna be your fairytale ending. He's gonna rip your heart out."

And I was going to rip out Ian's.

The certainty of it came on so suddenly that I grabbed my wine glass and downed the chardonnay in one gulp. Tense, inconsequential conversation filled the air during dinner—when we weren't immersed in uncomfortable silence. I emptied another glass of wine as Ian took care of the check.

Afterward, we ended up at a crowded dance club a few blocks from the restaurant where the music pulsed non-stop and the drinks flowed freely, though he cut me off after my third.

"Uh-uh, you're not getting drunk tonight. You're going to be in full control of yourself when I take you home." He palmed my ass and brought me tight against him as our bodies rocked to the rhythm. "And you're going to remember every second." His breath shuddered out against my neck, replaced an instant later by the pressure of his lips.

My blood pumped hard in my veins, and I held onto him to keep from melting to the dance floor. His erection pressed into my thigh as we moved together to the beat; he was more than ready to put action to words.

My head spun, from the alcohol, from the feel of his body against me. Heat and sexual tension smothered the air. "Can we get out of here?" Too many people closed in from all sides, and I wanted him alone. I wanted to lose myself, and I couldn't do that here.

"Hell, yes." He pulled me through the crowd, out the front entrance, and I sucked in fresh air until my lungs nearly burst with it. I was way too hot and it had everything to do with him.

He still got me going all right.

We covered the distance to his car in minutes, and soon we were speeding down the highway. He inched his hand up my leg, underneath my skirt, and slipped his fingers beyond the barrier of my panties. I parted my thighs and moaned as his touch sent tingles down my spine. He teased me the whole way home.

The car jerked into park in my driveway. He struck quickly, hauling me over the console and onto his lap. "Is this what you need? Someone burning up for you so much they can't make it to the door?" His mouth opened on my throat, hot and wet, and descended to my cleavage. "I want you so bad."

I leaned against the steering wheel, unmindful of the blast from the horn, and moaned as he yanked my top down over a breast. He sucked my aching nipple between his lips and grazed with his teeth.

I hissed in a breath. "We need to go inside."

He groaned. "I know, but I've waited so long to touch you like this again, to taste you." He lifted his head and gazed at me. "I still dream of that night. Still hear the breathless way you cried my name. I want to hear it again."

I reached for the handle and pushed the door open. "Take me inside." I untangled from his arms and found solid ground. He immediately drew me into his embrace as soon as he got to his feet. One hand tangled in my hair as he coaxed my mouth open under his. We slowly backed toward my front porch, unaware of anything but each other.

"It's locked," I moaned against his lips once we reached my porch.

"Give me the key." He never let go of me as I blindly dug in my purse with one hand. His lips traced a winding path down my neck.

"If you keep doing that, I'll never find it." Even as

the words left my mouth, I tilted my head so he'd continue.

He moved away with a sigh. "I'm not making love to you here on your doorstep, so find that key."

I finally pulled it from my purse and inserted the key, my fingers shaking. He picked me up, carried me inside, and the door slammed, echoing in my ears. He braced me against it and pressed his mouth against mine. His fingers inched under my camisole, sliding it above my breasts where his hands explored my tingling nipples.

"I love you so much," he said, inching back to look at me. "I'll never hurt you, never take you for granted or use you."

I couldn't say why, but his words brought tears to my eyes. "I'm wrong for you," I choked out.

He removed his hands from my breasts and framed my cheeks. "No, you're exactly right for me. You and I, we make sense. We always have."

Gage and I *didn't* make sense, so why was I suddenly consumed with thoughts of him? Ian's touch lit me on fire, but Gage's turned me into an inferno. His voice when he issued his commands, the way his eyes smoldered before he came—everything he did turned me to ash, and somehow he resurrected me every time.

The haze of passion I'd experienced at the club and in the car dissipated. "I can't do this," I whispered.

He leaned his forehead against mine. "Tell me why."

"You don't deserve this. I can't...I can't use you like this."

He sighed against my mouth. "Why do you think

you're using me?"

The truth stuck in my throat, like a piece of something I hadn't chewed all the way before swallowing. I dislodged it anyway and spoke the words I knew he didn't want to hear. The words I didn't want to admit to myself.

"Being with you makes me normal, and I…I'm not… normal." I squeezed my eyes shut. "The things he does to me—"

"He's sick, Kayla," he interrupted, an edge to his tone. "He's made you question who you are, and I *hate* him for that. There's nothing wrong with you! He should rot in jail for what he did."

I opened my eyes and drew in a shaky breath. "I'm sorry. This was a bad idea. I think you should leave."

"How did we go from kissing and touching"—he whispered before his lips claimed mine for a brief moment—"to arguing about him? He doesn't matter."

I shook my head and gently pushed against him. "He matters."

His shoulders drooped. "You won't let me try, will you? You'll let him do unspeakable things to you, but you won't let me in, not even a little."

The defeat in his tone tore at me. "Ian, you mean *so* much to me."

"But I'm not him."

"You're better than him. Better than me. I can't give you what you deserve. He…he wanted"—I gasped, trying to get the words out through the sobs rising in my throat —"to wreck you. Please," I begged, "don't let him." I wedged the door open. "Don't come back, don't call. Forget about me. I want you to move on and find someone who deserves you."

"Kayla"—his voice broke, and the sound alone bruised my heart—"*please…*"

"I won't sleep with you. That would be unforgivable of me. Go." I opened the door wider.

His hands fisted at his sides. "If I walk through that door, I'm not coming back."

"I…I know."

The next few moments were the longest of my life, but eventually he disappeared into the night, and I wasn't prepared for how his exit from my life broke my heart all over again.

6. TAKEN

I awoke to a crushing weight on my chest. Vise-like fingers encircled my wrists, rendering me incapable of moving, and a strangled cry tore from my throat. Instantly, I thought of Eve, but she wasn't here; she was with Stacey…

Oh God. No she wasn't. Stacey had dropped her off after Ian left. Someone had broken in, and she was asleep in the next room.

"Kayla!" A familiar voice said. "It's me. Calm down."

Gage.

I sucked in breaths of relief but then reality crept in again. What the hell was he doing in my bedroom in the middle of the night, pinning me to my mattress? He'd scared the life out of me until I'd realized he wasn't some random serial killer rapist. "What are you doing?" I squeaked. "If Eve wakes up, she'll be terrified. You can't pull shit like this!"

"Eve's safe."

I blinked, taking a moment to let his statement sink

in. "Of course she's *safe*. She's in her bed, Gage." My words came out too calmly for the panic fisting my heart.

"She's on her way to my jet. She's safe, Kayla."

"What the fuck do you mean she's on her way to your jet?" I fought against his hold, kicking and screaming, though his strength made my efforts useless. Gage had always been and always would be too strong for me. Tears heated my cheeks, though these were born of rage just as much as fear. "Why are you doing this?"

He wrenched my arms to the mattress and held them down, and his strong thighs kept mine from lifting off the bed. "I told you I wasn't leaving here without you, and I meant it. Now we can do this the easy way or the hard way. It's up to you, but if you want to be reunited with your daughter, then *don't fight me*." He loosened his grip slowly, as if testing to see if I'd attempt escape. "I'm going to let go, and you're going to get dressed, understand?"

With a gulp, I nodded. He let go and slid from the bed, and I got up on shaky legs, my breaths coming in choking gasps. I searched for the nearest pair of pants and pulled them on underneath my T-shirt.

"How can you do this to her? She must be terrified!" I wedged my feet into my sneakers and faced him, my body trembling. "I can't believe you kidnapped my daughter! Who has her? Please...you can't mess with Eve. She's innocent in all of this!" I fought the urge to get on my knees and beg, but doing so wouldn't help. He'd come this far and he wasn't about to change course now.

"She's fine. Katherine's with her."

Time did something funny. One instant I was standing a few feet from him, and the next I had my hands around his throat, squeezing as a red haze clouded my vision, fingernails digging in and scraping away skin until he yanked me out of reach from causing real harm. He twisted me, bent me over the bed, and used his thighs to trap me against the mattress. All the fight went out of me for a few seconds—seconds I couldn't afford because he used them to secure my hands behind my back.

"You're only making this harder on yourself."

"You fucking bastard!" How could he let that bitch anywhere near my daughter? I wanted to kill him; the urge to crush his throat with my bare hands overwhelmed me.

"Eve's fine, so knock it off. Katherine won't hurt her. She's a mother too."

And that was supposed to make it all better? I gritted my teeth as he pushed me into the hall where the narrow space seemed more suffocating than usual. Helplessness stole over me as we approached the front door. He was really doing this.

Why was I surprised?

Deep down, I never thought he'd involve Eve like this. He'd used her against me a year ago, but she'd been safe from the fallout. Safe as expected, considering she'd been fighting her own battle. But now…

He'd gone too far, even for Gage.

"I'll send movers for your things, but everything you need is already waiting." He grabbed my purse and keys before opening the door. "Let's go," he said, gesturing for me to go first.

How fucking gallant of him.

He didn't even bother to keep a physical hold on me; he knew he had me where it counted. He had Eve and that was enough to make me comply without hesitation. I slid into the passenger seat of his car and ignored the burn radiating down my arms from being restrained. He rounded the hood and settled into the driver's seat.

"Where are you taking me?"

"The airport, and if you promise to behave, I'll free your hands."

"Fuck you."

With a sigh, he started the ignition and pulled onto the street. "Have it your way."

"My way? How about you bring my daughter back and leave us the hell alone?"

He clenched his jaw. Keeping one hand on the steering wheel, he unzipped his pants with the other. "Get your head in my lap."

My eyes widened. I couldn't fight him, and he knew it all too well. He'd make me suck his cock all the way to the airport if he wanted, and there wasn't a damn thing I could do to stop him.

"I'll shut up now, I promise."

"Yes," he said, grasping my hair and jerking me sideways into his lap, "you will. Open that sweet mouth, Kayla." He wound my hair tight around his fist so I couldn't move and forced his erection between my lips. His taste flooded my senses and an unwanted response traveled through my body, like sparks misfiring.

My body had to be misfiring. No way was I getting off on this. He bobbed my head up and down, painfully yanking my hair as he neared release.

"Deeper." His command floated above me, a breathless whisper as the road sped underneath us. To his credit, I didn't sense the car swerving at all, but that was Gage—always in control.

He pushed into my throat and came in a gush. "Swallow," he said, holding my head down to the point of smothering me. I couldn't *not* swallow.

Neither of us spoke afterward. I was too busy gulping in air as he dabbed at my mouth and chin with a napkin. I tried lifting my head, but he refused to let me up. His penis went flaccid against my cheek, and my tears drenched his lap as I cried myself into a doze.

The soothing hum of the highway was absent when he woke me. I struggled into a sitting position and noticed his jet through eyes bleary from sleep. No one witnessed him escorting me onto that monstrous machine with my hands tied behind my back.

Even the pilot turned a blind eye once we boarded.

Katherine didn't. I expected her usual smugness, but something close to uncertainty pinched her face as she took in my restrained hands. She sat next to Eve, who lay sprawled on the couch at the front of the jet, fast asleep.

"Gage, I can't go to jail over this!" Katherine cried. "You didn't tell me you were kidnapping her."

"Lower your voice." He was so calm it was irritating. "Let's not wake Eve." He gave Katherine a pointed glare and then turned to me, as if her presence was of little importance to him. "If I untie you, will you behave? I'd rather not have a scene in front of your daughter."

Caging my anger, I nodded. He released my hands, and I rubbed my wrists until I got some circulation back. The severity of what he'd done hit me, and I was an instant away from panicking again. He pushed me onto the couch and took the cushion beside me. I wanted to go to Eve, but Katherine sat between my daughter and me, and Gage slid an arm around my shoulders anyway, keeping me at his side. His hold was just as possessive as always. I peeked up and got a spark of satisfaction upon seeing the nasty red scratches I'd left on his neck and throat.

As the jet sped down the runway and took to the air, I thought of only one thing.

He's gone too far this time.

7. RETURN OF THE MASTER

The flight was shorter than expected. We beat the sunrise as we landed in Portland, not that we would have seen much of it anyway with the way the sky was crying. Now the four of us entered Gage's house. He shut and locked the door before turning to Katherine. "Take Eve to her room and sit with her. It's the last door on the right."

She gritted her teeth but went to do as ordered. Eve opened her eyes and looked over Katherine's shoulder, calling to me.

"It's okay." My voice cracked. "Go back to sleep, baby. She'll tuck you in." Comforted by my voice and words, she laid her cheek down, and I watched them disappear down the hall.

Gage clutched my arm. "Come on."

"Please stop," I begged, fighting our progress toward that door—the door leading to the one place I never wanted to see again. "Gage, don't do this to me."

Ignoring me, he inserted a key and the door creaked open, revealing the darkness beyond. I remembered how it infiltrated every corner, every implement of torture. Gage was at his darkest when in that space.

"You said you loved me," I cried. He pushed me in front of him, and through my panic I heard the door slam and the lock click into place.

"I do, Kayla. So fucking much."

He switched on a light and herded me down the steps. "Strip."

"No," I said, folding my arms.

He took a deep breath and seemed to deliberate for a moment. "You have no options. The only way through that door is by key. Now strip. I want you bare in front of me."

"Why?"

"Just do it." His tone was free of anger, free of anything other than resignation, and I wasn't sure what it meant.

I slipped off my shoes and brought my trembling fingers to the hem of my shirt. I wasn't wearing a bra, and his eyes glazed over at the sight of my breasts, nipples puckering in the chill of the room. I pushed my pants down my legs, followed by my underwear, and stepped outside the puddle of clothing to stand before him, reduced to a shivering mass of vulnerability.

This was about more than stripping me of my clothes.

"What do you want, Gage?"

"Every damn piece of you."

"Even my daughter?"

"Even your daughter."

I dropped to my knees from the force of his words. "Let us go!"

His tall frame became a blur through my tears, and I was unprepared for the ball gag he shoved deep into my mouth. He wrenched my hands up and secured them. His movements were measured but quick, and I had no time to adjust to what he was doing. He hauled me to my feet and kicked my legs apart, and I never thought I'd end up back here again—in Gage's basement of hell, strung up on my toes, hands secured above me and feet spread wide.

I'd come full circle, and I didn't like it one bit. Unlike last time, when fear and uncertainty had taken center stage, now an all-consuming rage filled my soul. I *hated* being helpless and at his mercy, rendered incapable of expressing the fury boiling in the vat of my being.

He had Eve, and no one messed with my daughter. Not even Gage Fucking Channing.

He sank into a seat, lowered his head into his hands, and didn't speak at first—just gripped his hair with those slender fingers that still managed to deliver lethal masculinity, as if he could hold himself together. Minutes passed. He didn't move, and I *couldn't* move.

What did he want?

"I have something to say, and you're going to listen," he said, rising from the couch and pacing in front of me. "I didn't want to do this. I tried doing the right thing, tried giving you time to come to me on your own, but then you fucked him." He stopped, and his face twisted, reminding me of how furious he'd been a year ago after catching me in Ian's arms the first time.

I jerked my head back and forth, trying to convey his mistake, but he didn't take out the gag and listen. His actions made sense now, knowing Gage the way I did. He thought I'd slept with Ian and now his jealousy had sent him off the deep end. I had to get through to him. Had to tell him he was wrong.

Some of my anger seeped from my limbs, leaving me shaking with weakness, and for the first time since he'd kidnapped me, I truly feared him. He had everything wrong, but he'd left me incapable of correcting his assumption. God. What would he do to me now?

He wouldn't hurt Eve…

I thought the words, turned them over in my mind, but a spark of doubt remained. He was too unpredictable in his jealousy. Especially when he appeared calm.

And he was calm. This was bad. I screamed around the gag.

"Damn it, Kayla! Don't look at me like that." I broke out in a cold sweat when he unbuckled his belt. "I'm going to prove I can get angry—fucking furious even— and still punish you without losing control." Brandishing that painful strap of leather, he disappeared behind me.

How did I get back here?

A year without physical pain had weakened me. His first strike purged more tears from my eyes, and the second lash crashed on top of the first, back to back, leaving me no time to acclimate to the overwhelming sting. I cried out in muffled abandon with each strike, and by the time he ceased hitting me, my legs were gelatinous, and I was sinking…

He released my hands, and I collapsed to my knees. I peered up through my messy hair, plastered to my face from sweat and tears, and met his guarded expression. Something lingered in his eyes. Hurt?

Was it even possible to hurt him?

"I'm no good for you," he said. "He's fucking perfect for you. He'll give you the idyllic life, white picket fence and all with two-point-five kids. I can give you anything and everything, but I can't give you that. I don't do *normal*." His hands bunched as he came toward me. "But I can't let you go either. You're under my skin, in my head. I dream of you when I sleep and it's making me crazy." His eyes narrowed, alight with the emotion he didn't want to spill. "I want to kill him for touching what's mine, and whether you like it or not, you are mine. Your body knows it, and I think your heart does too."

I brought my hands up and pulled out the gag. "I didn't sleep with him!"

He dropped to his knees in front of me, and his hands came up to frame my cheeks. At first, his touch was gentle, but as he brought his face closer, he dug his fingers into my skin. "You better consider your next words carefully, because if you lie to me about this—"

"It's the truth," I interrupted. "I didn't sleep with him."

"I saw you guys. You were all over each other and barely made it through the fucking door."

"Obviously, you didn't stick around." I jerked back until his hands dropped. "I made him leave."

His mouth claimed mine, hard and insistent. I whimpered, but he ate it up, leaving me to question if I'd made any sound at all. He pulled away and searched my face. "You promise you didn't sleep with him?"

"Yes," I said, tears still streaming down my face. "I couldn't. It didn't feel right."

"But when we're together…it feels right, doesn't it?"

I choked on my answer.

"Do you love me, Kayla?"

"It doesn't matter what I feel. I can't live like this! You can't just do whatever you want because you're jealous."

He shook his head. "I won't live without you, so I guess that leaves you with two options. One, you can fight me every step of the way, but you're still not leaving. Or there's option two."

"What's option two?"

"You can accept we're meant to be together and compromise with me."

I arched a brow. "You, compromise?"

"Yes. Compromising isn't something I do easily, but I love you enough that I'd do it for you."

I scoffed. "How nice. You'll be a decent human being because you love me. Are you listening to yourself? Does any of this really penetrate your thick skull? This"—I gestured between him and me—"isn't normal! You don't treat someone you love like this. This here…this is a watered down version of what Rick put me through. Why would I go back to that?"

"Don't you *ever* compare me to that piece of shit again. I might hurt you, but I'll never harm you."

"But you do harm me. Every time you take the choice from me, and I'll be damned if I let your methods corrupt my daughter. I want her to know what love is. If I stay with you, she'll grow up believing this is how relationships are supposed to be."

"No," he said in a level tone. "We'll contain the more unconventional aspects of our relationship to our bedroom and down here. She'll never be exposed to anything inappropriate. I'll protect her. I'll protect you too. No one will ever hurt you again, including me."

My gaze dropped to the front of his pants where his belt had been moments ago. "What do you call beating me?"

"Punishment." He slipped his fingers between my legs. "Your wet cunt suggests my belt isn't such a punishment after all. I'll have to come up with more interesting methods."

Every part of me tingled at his touch. I didn't have the energy to deny it. Everything this man did turned me on, and I'd long ago forgotten whether he'd conditioned the response from me, or if it had been there all along.

There were no more lines; they'd blurred until nothing but pixilated confusion remained.

He rose, picked up his belt from the floor, and wound it through his pant loops. I silently watched as he crossed the room where he pulled out a silky robe from a closet. Sticking out a hand, he helped me to my feet and held the garment open for me to slide my arms into. His fingers tangled with mine as he led me to the couch.

"Now, let's talk boundaries," he said after we were

sitting side by side.

"I'm listening." I'd hear him out, and then I'd get the hell out of there with Eve the first chance I got.

"I need to know your hard limits."

I reached into the vault of my memory and tried to recall the research I'd done into BDSM last year. "Hard limits…those are things that won't be done under any circumstances, right?"

"Yes."

My gaze swerved to the wall where he kept his paddles and whips. The sight of the long and thin one, coiled against the wall like a lethal snake, sent terror into me despite his efforts to use it without anger. That night replayed in my mind, and I grew even wetter between my thighs. He'd done something to me that night.

The night I'd gone to him on my own.

But that whip…

"I don't want whips or paddles. Your belt"—I swallowed hard—"is my limit, as long as you don't use it when you're mad."

His attention landed on the whip too, and he frowned. "You're scared of the bullwhip." With a sigh, he dragged his fingers through his hair. "That's my fault. I wish I could take back what I did, but I can't." He paused, seeming to consider. "Okay. No bullwhip. We'll revisit this conversation in a few months. Maybe you'll change your mind by then."

I doubted it, but I remained silent.

"What else, Kayla?"

"Nipple clamps."

"Absolutely not. Those aren't going anywhere."

"Why?" I cocked my head and studied him. I was genuinely curious.

"They look sexy as fuck on you."

They also hurt like hell. "I don't like them."

He lowered his hands to my chest, parted the robe, and his eyes wandered over my breasts. I stopped breathing when he bent and sucked a nipple into his mouth.

"Gage…" Just like that, he stole my breath and the last bit of composure I had left. I fisted my hands until my nails bit into my palms. "No clamps," I mumbled, though my demand would have carried more weight if I hadn't said it with a moan.

He pulled back, and his eyes rose to meet mine. "This is called compromising. Bullwhip or clamps—you only get one as a hard limit."

I bit my lip. The clamps hurt, but the whip terrified me. "This isn't compromising. You're using my fear against me to get your way."

"Okay, the clamps will only be used as punishment."

"You're an asshole."

His mouth quirked into a grin. "Calling me names might constitute a punishment."

"I stand by my previous observation. I don't even know why we're having this conversation. You'll always get what you want."

He tilted his head. "True. But I do care what you want too. So no bullwhips, and clamps used sparingly. Now what else?"

"I want to see my daughter."

"Soon. What else?"

I opened my mouth, prepared to mention all kinds of horrible things I didn't want, but when I thought back to every moment I'd spent with him, nothing formed. My mind was a blank canvas, unnerving me so deeply that I shuddered. Why couldn't I remember the bad?

Why was the good—the *unbelievably* good—running through my mind like a hot porno? And then it hit me.

"No anal sex."

He laughed. "No deal."

I sprang to my feet and glared at him. "Then rape me again, Gage, because that's what you'll have to do. I'm done with this conversation. I've told you my limits, but you've shot down almost every one of them." I crossed my arms. "What's the point?"

He rose to his full height and stood close enough so his breath warmed my face, and his eyes smoldered in that familiar way—the way that made me fear and want him all at once. I tensed, waiting for him to grab me and force me to the bed. I was in for it now, since the subject of anal had precipitated this particular standoff.

He leaned down, and I thought he was going to kiss me, but he spoke instead. "No anal," he said, inches from my mouth. "No anal until you beg me for it."

"That will never happen."

"We'll see." He snaked an arm around my waist and pulled me against him. "I think we've covered hard limits. Now let's talk about what you *do* like."

Oh God.

I gulped. So not going there now. "I want to see Eve."

"Okay, we'll continue this conversation later. Maybe you can *show* me what you like, though I already have a few ideas." His mouth brushed mine, barely a touch but enough to make my pulse thready. "You're anxious to see your daughter, and I can understand that." He inched back, and his expression grew severe. New flutters of dread winged in my stomach. "But I need you to say yes to something before I let you through that door, Kayla."

"Wh…what is it?"

He reached into his pocket and withdrew a velvet box, and when he flipped the lid open, I thought I'd pass out. "I want you to marry me."

"No!" I shoved away from him, stumbling as my grip on sanity teetered. "You're insane. I'm not marrying you!"

He avoided eye contact as he shut the ring box. I couldn't even recall what the stone had looked like—my mind was too hazed with shock.

"I'm not letting you out of here until you say yes."

"You wouldn't." He'd never terrified me so much. "What would you do with Eve?"

"Let's hope you never find out." He strode toward the staircase, and I hurried after him, desperation fueling every step.

"Don't do this! She needs me." Tears threatened again, but I held them back. He didn't respond to them anyway. Not in a way that was favorable to me.

He whirled to face me. "If you come anywhere near these stairs, I'll tie you to the bed before I leave."

My body froze. "Please, I'm begging you, Gage."

"It's Master. When we're down here or in our bedroom, you'll address me as Master."

Like hell I would.

"Get some sleep," he barked. "I'll bring in lunch later, and hopefully by then you'll have changed your mind."

8. YES

The day commenced with the biggest standoff of my life. He brought in lunch, opened that little dreaded box, and then promptly shut it and left without a word after I said no. The same thing happened at dinnertime. He wouldn't budge, and he refused to engage in conversation despite my pleading, so negotiating was out of the question.

Most disturbing of all? He didn't touch me, even though the heat in his eyes told me how badly he wanted to. His restraint said it all. I was screwed. He was being stubbornly serious about this, and I'd lost our battle of wills before it had begun. When it came to Eve, I'd already proven I'd do anything for her.

The sound of his entrance the next morning made my heart speed up.

"You can eat breakfast down here by yourself, or you can join Eve and me. It's your choice," he said as he pulled the ring box from his pocket. "Are you ready to say yes?"

No, not even close, but being away from Eve was

killing me, and I couldn't stand the thought of how scared she must be wondering where I was. I'd do anything to get to her, even let Gage put a ring on my finger if it meant he'd let me out of this damn room.

"I'll marry you."

I was unprepared for the grin that widened his mouth; it wasn't smug, triumphant, or even cocky. I felt that unrestrained smile in the pit of my stomach. My answer made him *happy*.

Genuinely so, and I wasn't sure how I felt about that.

His hand slid along mine as he pushed the ring onto my finger, and God, it was gigantic. The diamond, a princess cut, sparkled in a beautiful antique setting. He gathered me into his arms and buried his nose in my hair.

"I can't wait to get you in bed underneath me. I've missed you so damn much."

I sucked in a breath and held it. He finally released me, took my hand, and pulled me toward the stairs.

Eve's eyes lit up the instant she saw me. She hopped into my arms with her usual exuberance. "I missed you. Are you all better now?"

I sent Gage a confused look.

"I explained to her how you weren't feeling well."

"Yeah, baby. I'm better now." My eyes stung as I held her tight. I was so much better now that I had her in my arms.

"Come see my room!" She slid down my body, and her feet pitter-pattered across the sheen of hardwood. I sensed Gage's presence behind me as I followed her down a hallway, past the master bedroom I couldn't bring myself to look into, and when I rounded the door frame to the next room, I stood motionless, my mouth hanging open.

The room was a four-year-old's dream come true. A canopy bed enclosed in filmy tulle sat along one wall, and shelves upon shelves of toys and books took up another. Every nook and cranny overflowed with the princess theme.

The bastard had bought my daughter, but what really unsettled me was the evidence in front of me; he'd planned this.

I clenched my hands and tried to contain my anger. I couldn't compete, and she'd be so disappointed to go back to our life, assuming I could find a way out of there in the first place.

"Do you like it, Mommy?"

"It's very...nice."

"Look at the pretty tea cups!" She shot across the room to a table in the corner and lifted a dainty cup from its saucer. "Will you play tea party with me?"

"I will in a few minutes. I have to talk to Gage first." I backed into the hall and moved out of earshot of Eve. His presence filled the narrow space, and the shadows the early morning sun hadn't yet chased away only added to the threatening undertone of this situation, this moment. I made myself stand tall as I faced him.

"How dare you!"

He moved toward me, and instinctively, I backed away until my spine hit wall. "How dare I what? Make her happy? Give her things? She's had a blast since she's been here, despite missing you."

"You know I can't give her all of that." My voice shook, so I took a deep breath. "How will I explain all of this after we…"

"After you what?" He aligned his body with mine. "Leave? Entertaining thoughts of skipping out on me, are you? Even though you're wearing my mother's ring."

His words carried special weight, as if they meant something…something I was supposed to understand? But I didn't. I was floundering in a sea of turbulence, the waters deep and murky so the unknown remained just that.

He brought my left hand to his mouth and kissed the ring. "You're not going anywhere," he murmured. He pulled away but flattened his palms against the wall on either side of me.

He was right. I wasn't going anywhere, not even from this hallway.

"How long do you plan to keep us prisoner?"

"As long as it takes."

"You can't keep us locked away forever. Eve needs to be in preschool, and she's in remission. She has appointments—"

"You think I don't realize that? I'm aware you have obligations as a mother, but if I have to, I can hire someone to transport her." He leaned closer. "But I don't think it'll take long. I think you're exactly where you want to be."

"You're overly confident," I snapped, focusing on his chest even though I felt his gaze burning into me.

"And you're in denial." His hands smoothed over my cheeks before slipping into my hair. He tilted my head up. "You wouldn't have sent him away if you didn't feel this too."

My lids closed to the softness of his tone because the sight of him amplified everything. His lips pressed against mine, and our mouths opened, tongues sliding together slowly. He took his time kissing me, as if making up for the last twenty-four hours he'd gone without touching me.

I came back to myself sometime later, my hands fisted in his hair as his pelvis rocked with mine, and I thought of Eve's proximity. We needed to be more responsible; in fact, we needed to be more responsible in general. "If you intend to keep me here—"

"I *am* keeping you here." He lifted me and urged my legs around his waist. "And I'm going to sink into your body every night."

"Then we need to talk about birth control."

"What about it?"

"We didn't use any in Texas."

He paused. "I guess we didn't."

I moaned as he ground his erection into me. "We can't be so reckless."

"I'll get you a prescription today," he said, hips still rocking. At this point, our clothing was the only thing stopping us.

Eve.

I didn't want her witnessing something so inappropriate. I pushed against him until he let me down.

"Not here. Eve's—"

"I know," he interrupted, his chest heaving. "Later. Go spend some time with your daughter. I'll make breakfast."

He stepped away, but I grasped his hand. "Wait...is Katherine still here?" The thought of facing her again was more than I could stand.

"No. She left yesterday."

"What is she to you?" Why had I asked that? I didn't want to know, didn't want to hear about her at all, but the question had nagged me since I'd seen her on the plane.

"She's nothing. She doesn't matter."

"She matters, Gage. You entrusted my daughter to her. Damn right she matters."

Gage's mouth flattened into a hard line. "We have an...understanding."

I narrowed my eyes. "What kind of understanding?"

"She helps me, and I help her fight her ex in court for custody of their son. Everyone wins."

Except for Eve and me. We didn't win.

I watched him disappear down the hall, and I waited a few moments before creeping after him. If I remembered correctly, I couldn't get to the front door without walking in direct sight of the kitchen. I peeked around the corner, and he stared right at me.

"Need something?"

I shook my head. The quirk of his mouth told me he knew what I was up to, and I said the first thing that came to mind. "Can you make pancakes? She loves them." I turned to join Eve, but his voice stopped me.

"You won't get around me, Kayla. I won't let my guard down."

Neither will I.

But I was lying to myself. The minute he got me in bed, he'd have me.

9. LOVE ME

The three of us spent the day together watching movies and playing games. It was the oddest sight ever, seeing Gage crouched on the floor playing something as elementary as Candy Land. Witnessing how Eve responded to him disturbed me on all kinds of levels. He kept up a constant stream of chatter with her that night during dinner, as if he talked to kids on a daily basis. He asked about her favorite shows, if she knew how to sing her ABC's; he even asked what she wanted for her birthday, though that was still a couple months away.

He was using her innocence to worm his way into her heart, and I could do nothing to stop it. Not unless I wanted to cause a scene in front of Eve, which I didn't. He cleaned up after dinner while I gave her a bath, and afterward, as I tucked her into bed, he lingered in the doorway watching us. I wasn't ready to leave her alone yet, but even more so, I wasn't ready to be alone with *him*.

"Do we live here now? I like my room." Her question was so guileless, it broke my heart.

I forced a smile. "We'll see. Goodnight, baby." My gaze darted to Gage. "I'll be in the next room, okay?"

She nodded as she sank into her blankets, and her eyes fluttered closed. I turned on the nightlight before shutting off the overhead light. Gage led me down the hall, and we stopped in front his bedroom—the room he expected me to share with him. I couldn't fathom calling that space ours.

"What if she wakes up?" I asked.

"I installed monitors in our room and down in the basement. We'll hear her." His gaze wandered down my body. "I have to take care of a few things in my office first," he said, pointing to another door at the mouth of the hallway. "I'll leave the door open."

I didn't miss the warning in his tone. He'd always be watching me; that much was clear.

"There's a private bath off the master suite. Prepare for me. When you're done, I expect you on your knees waiting."

"And if I don't?"

"I'll punish you." He smiled as his attention dropped to my chest. "I wouldn't mind seeing your nipples clamped and aching. You think the ones I used last year were bad? I have worse sets."

Just like that, he'd transitioned me back into the role of submissive. I shrank into myself, keeping my eyes downcast as the sheer presence of his body closed in.

"Wait for me on your knees, thighs spread and hands behind your back." His breath heated my forehead. "I want you naked. Understand?"

I nodded.

"How do you address me, Kayla?"

"Master is my safe word."

"Like hell it is."

I raised my eyes to his. "You got what you want. You have me here following your orders, but I won't call you Master. So beat me, rape me, show me how ugly you can get. I'll never call you that again."

His eyes narrowed. "You did the other night."

"What are you talking about?"

"In Texas, when we were fucking, you called me Master."

I reached into my memories and recalled the word slipping from my traitorous lips. "I was caught up in the moment."

His grin was positively evil. "So if we're 'in the moment,' and you utter that word because you want to come so badly, should that be my cue to stop since that's your safe word?"

I bit down on my tongue to keep from coming unglued. He was the most infuriating man I'd ever known. "You mentioned compromising."

He gave a slight nod. "I did."

"Can we at least compromise on this?"

He leaned into me. "What do you have in mind?"

"I'll call you Master when we're…"

"Say it. Fucking."

"I'll call you Master when we're *fucking*." That word struck me as all kinds of wrong. What we did transcended a casual coupling, despite my protests to the contrary.

"But you have a name, and I'll use it."

"I *am* your Master. You don't have to say the word—we both know it's true." He smirked. "Wait for me on your knees. I don't care how long it takes. Don't move from that position until I say otherwise." He backed away a couple of steps. "I bet you're getting wet just thinking about it."

"You're an asshole." But he was right. I *was* getting achingly warm between my legs.

"And you need to be punished. I'll be in shortly." He turned and strode down the hall.

I stumbled into the room on jittery limbs and entered the private bath. He'd be a while. I was almost sure of it, so I took my time in grooming for him. Like a good little slave.

God, what the hell am I doing here?

He hadn't left me with any other choice, but at the same time…I wasn't fighting him as hard as I could be. I shaved every inch of my legs and worked on my bikini area. Afterward, I pulled a brush through my thick locks.

And then I surrendered to his demands.

I kept my hands clasped behind me and thighs spread, and the floor became uncomfortable beneath my knees. Cool air drifted between them, igniting more heat in the place he owned. My nipples pebbled in the chilly room.

He was going to clamp them. I'd mouthed off to him one too many times, and now I'd pay the price. I almost groaned at the thought. Why couldn't he fuck me like a normal man?

Normal doesn't get you off so good.

So it was true; I was a masochist after all.

Even though I was waiting for him, I jumped when he pushed the door open. "Close your eyes," he demanded.

My lids fluttered closed, and I strained to hear him, picking up his quiet steps as he neared me. He covered my eyes with a satiny piece of cloth.

"Part your lips."

My mouth opened, breath escalating at the sound of his tone, which sparked through me like fireworks.

He pressed on my lower lip before slipping a finger inside to stroke my tongue. "Don't speak, and I won't gag you. I know you don't like when I do that, so I won't as long as you behave. But you will get the clamps. I won't stand for you disrespecting me."

His finger left my mouth, and he gently rolled a nipple between thumb and forefinger. His caress made me ache so intensely that I almost begged him to take me. His touch was a tease at first until he pinched hard. He applied the most excruciating clamp imaginable, and I managed to remain silent until he did the same to the other side.

I cried out and jerked away. "I'm sorry! I didn't mean —"

He pressed a finger against my mouth. "Don't move. Don't make a sound. When I'm ready to remove them, I'll remove them, but not a second sooner. Endure it, Kayla, and the next time you have the urge to call me 'asshole,' you'll remember this pain."

Asshole.

If I didn't rebel vocally, at least I could silently. I remained still as the dead and sensed him standing before me the entire time, his eyes on the vises that caused me so much pain but turned him on all the more. My eyes stung and watered, and after a while my nipples went numb.

It was going to hurt like hell when he removed them.

He did so without warning, and I bit my lip hard to keep quiet as pain flooded my sensitive peaks. He slipped a hand between my legs. "See? Not nearly as wet as you were after I used my belt on you. This is definitely a more effective punishment."

"Gage?"

"Yes?"

"We never established a safe word."

"Pick one now."

"Um...I can't think of one."

"Then we'll use yellow and red. Yellow means you're uncomfortable with what I'm doing and you want me to slow down. Red means stop so we can assess."

"Okay."

"Doesn't apply to punishments though. You don't get a safe word during those."

Of course I didn't. Had I expected otherwise? The sound of his clothing whispered to the floor, and I wished I could see him. His finger wedged between my lips and pushed down until my jaw went slack.

"Keep your mouth parted just like that." The wet tip of his cock tickled my tongue, and his taste brought back all kinds of memories; mostly of fear and hatred, overshadowed by intense desire. He bathed my lips with his moisture, and I didn't know if he was going to fuck my mouth like he had so many times in the past, or if he only intended to tease.

"We never discussed introducing new things. We'll try them, and if you're uncomfortable, you can tell me later, but you can't deny me something until we've tried it."

Nervous tension spread through me. What was he proposing now? And I was getting sick of him making up the rules as he went along.

"What do you—"

He shoved his cock all the way in. "I'm going to come on your face." He slipped in and out of my mouth, quick and rough, and his ragged breathing roared in my ears. I didn't have time to process what he intended—didn't have time to agree or disagree. I gagged as he pushed deep, and he came in a rapid burst. Some of his cum hit the back of my throat before he yanked out of my mouth. He pulled the blindfold from my eyes, and his thick and warm liquid flowed over my forehead, down my nose and cheeks, and lingered on my lips. I darted my tongue out to clean them.

"Fuck, that's a sight. My cum all over that gorgeous face of yours." He gazed at me, entranced for several moments before helping me to my feet. "Go clean up, then crawl to me on your hands and knees."

I scurried into the bathroom, my pulse thrumming at my collarbone. I didn't recognize the woman in the mirror. She looked insanely aroused with her face and lips damp from the essence of him, her eyes mud brown with want.

I wasn't me anymore. I hadn't been me for a very long time. He'd taken what was left and had locked it away somewhere in the vault of his possession. I lifted my left hand, wiggled my fingers, and stared at the rock. He was steamrolling me again. Compromise didn't exist between us; he was getting exactly what he wanted.

"Kayla, hurry up!"

I splashed cool water on my face, dried off with a towel, and then got to my hands and knees. Cold tile smoothed into hardwood as I left the bathroom. Maybe I could talk him into putting carpet in; these floors were killing me. I glanced up as I crawled to him.

"Eyes on the floor."

Lowering my head, I watched my hands take me closer to him, ring sparkling from the light overhead. His bare feet came into view, and I stalled in that spot, staring at his beautiful feet. Everything about him appealed to me, and I hated it.

"Kiss my feet, Kayla."

The fucked up part about this? I leaned down and did so without a second thought.

"You are mine. You follow my commands so well. I bet if I brought out the bullwhip, you'd take it right now."

He was probably right. I was lost in my desire for him, but I still managed to utter two words. "You promised."

"And I keep my promises. No bullwhip. But I am your Master. Just because you refuse to say the word doesn't mean you don't think it, don't act on it." He stepped back a few feet. "Put your nose to the floor and spread your arms out in front of you."

I stretched my body, nose to the floor, in the ultimate pose of submission.

"You're so fucking gorgeous. God, Kayla, get up. I need you so bad right now I'm about to explode."

I got to my feet, and he swept me into his arms. The light went out an instant before he crawled over me on the bed. I sank into the soft mattress, and we meshed together, naked body against naked body as he cradled my face in his hands. I breathed in his breath and tasted my own need.

"Kayla," he said before dropping his forehead to mine. "I've fucked you all kinds of ways, but tonight...I just want to love you."

"Then love me," I choked. A tear trickled down my cheek. His words filled me up so much. I gasped for air, overcome by it all, by the sensation of his body against mine, our hearts beating in sync. He was like several people rolled into one, but right at this moment, this version of him had me.

I was his forever.

"Do you forgive me?" he asked.

"I...I'm trying."

"Do you love me?"

"I'm trying not to."

"You're good at obeying me, so try less hard on that second point."

He raised my arms over my head, and his fingers trailed down the sides of my breasts as he kissed a wet path to my navel, over the scars of my past. "I could murder him for doing this to you." His fingers brushed over my stab wounds. "You're still perfection though." He swirled his tongue there, but I felt his kiss everywhere.

Another tear leaked out; he was cleansing me of the pain I'd carried with me for so long. "Don't break my heart, Gage."

"I'll protect your heart." He kissed his way south, down my thighs until he reached my knees. He placed a kiss on each one before pushing them apart, and I shivered as his breath fanned over me. "Come as many times as you need to. Don't wait, don't ask for permission. You have it." His fingers entered me first, followed by the intense heat of his mouth claiming me. I wrapped my fingers around the bars of the headboard and moaned.

He'd never made me come this way before, and I wanted it so badly—wanted my taste flooding *his* senses. His tongue circled, once, twice, three times, and I cried his name. He spiraled a finger inside me, plunging deeper. The headboard shook as I held on, my body arching… arching until I thought I'd break. Still, he didn't stop.

My legs trembled, cramped, and I bucked my hips in desperation, wanting more his mouth, more of his fingers. More of *him*. I couldn't stop. I didn't want to stop. The slide of his tongue felt incredibly good, so hot and wet and making me throb from the heels of my feet to the top of my head. I was about to fly apart underneath him.

And then he did the unthinkable. He stopped.

"Oh God! Don't stop!" I was a mess, tears drenching my face, body shaking, heart racing way ahead of me, and he was fucking *stopping*? "Please, I'm begging you. Love me."

"I do," he said, his voice floating to me on a hoarse whisper. "Say it."

"Say what? Damn it, Gage!" I raised my hips toward him, but he didn't put his mouth on me again.

"Who am I?"

I lifted my head and saw the shadow of him crouched between my knees, like a predator about to feast. "You're my damn Master! You own me, body, mind, soul. Please…God…don't stop." Out of breath, I collapsed against the mattress again, and when his tongue burrowed into my sex, I screamed and shattered. My hands left the headboard and fisted his hair, holding him to me like a greedy whore.

But I was his whore. Just his. Only his.

He crawled up my body, and his arms enfolded me as he slipped inside, agonizingly slow. He wasn't in a hurry this time, wasn't a beast driven by his wants and needs. The connection between us terrified and confused me, left me in awe of this brutal yet passionate man who turned me to liquid with his touch. He gripped my face, and his kiss reached the center of my being as our bodies moved together. God, he owned me in that kiss.

"Come for me again," he whispered, breaking our lip-lock and settling his head on my chest. "It's the sexiest sound ever, baby."

Another orgasm was already building, rushing through the dam he'd broken, and I cried out in short, breathless whimpers with each unhurried thrust. Warmth flooded where our bodies connected, and the heat seemed to span from here until never.

Oh God...Oh God...

"You feel so amazing," he said, burying his face in my breasts. "I'll never get enough." With one final plunge, he tensed and groaned my name.

And the truth hit me with the force of a hurricane. He was making love to me. This wasn't about fucking, wasn't about claiming or possessing me.

This was about loving me.

10. AFTERGLOW

We lay together afterward, a twisted bundle of limbs. His hands never stopped touching or stroking, and I realized once you got beyond the darkness in him, the whips and pain, he was the most sensual man alive.

"Still awake?" he asked.

"Yeah." I let out a huge yawn.

His chest rumbled underneath my cheek in laughter. "Barely."

"You worked me over good."

"The working over was mutual, Kayla."

A question rose but caught in my throat. I swallowed and forced it from my lips. "Why me?"

He fell silent for so long, I was certain he had no intention of answering. "I didn't want to want you."

I could relate.

He drew lazy circles up and down my spine. "You got to me. I noticed how much you loved your daughter..." He heaved in a breath. "I don't want to talk about this right now."

"Gage, I just want—"

"Not now," he barked.

I flinched, and he let out a sigh. "I'm always going to fuck up. I've got a horrible temper." He paused. "But you already know that. You know that better than anyone." He hauled me on top of his lap and brought my left leg over his right thigh so I straddled him.

My head fell back, mouth open though no sound escaped, as I pushed down onto his cock. He rocked into me, slow and steady.

"How could you hurt me like that?" I gasped as he pushed higher.

The glow from the clock on the nightstand illuminated his expression. He closed his eyes, and his face tensed, as if he were in pain. "I looked at you and all I saw was him."

"What do you see now, Gage?" I lifted and slid down his smooth shaft, inch by inch.

He groaned, and his eyes opened but remained hooded. "I see this incredible, sexy woman who belongs to me." He plastered his hands on my breasts. "Only me."

His possessiveness shouldn't have sent me over the edge, but it did. I collapsed onto his heaving chest afterward, slick with sweat and spent, but still yearning for answers.

"You said it's your mother's ring. Are the two of you close?"

"We were, before she died."

Something clicked, and I recalled Ian mentioning her death years ago. "Cancer, right?" I said, my chest squeezing the breath from me.

"She passed a few months after Liz." He paused, his Adam's apple moving as he swallowed hard, and I sensed him shutting down. "People die, Kayla."

"Tell me about Liz," I pressed.

"I don't talk about her."

Each time we were together, he stole another piece of me. I wanted the same from him. Answers. An idea of what made him tick. Was that too much to ask?

"You want this to work between us. You want me to stay and marry you, but you give me nothing in return. That's hardly fair."

"I gave you three orgasms tonight. That's hardly nothing."

Even though I heard the amusement in his tone, his words still irritated.

"You've taken everything from me," I said. "You literally turned my world on its head."

"I haven't taken everything. Not yet."

"What are you talking about?"

"Your heart. You still hold it close, still guard it."

"Can you blame me?"

He didn't answer right away. "No."

I lifted my head. "Gage? I...you..."

"Tell me."

"You have my heart."

He drew my face to his, and our lips met. "You still haven't said what I want to hear."

"You still haven't told me about Liz."

"You don't quit, do you?"

"Do you?" I countered. "You push and push until you get what you want. I've learned from the best."

His hands fell from my body. "She was my first. First everything. I was so fucking angry all the time, and she taught me how to let it out, introduced me to the deviant side of sex. We connected, understood each other."

"How did you find out about her and…"

"Say his name." The steel in his voice made me cringe. "If you can't even say his name, then we have a problem. I'll go mad knowing you still love him."

"I care about him, but I was so young when we were together, and we were barely together, Gage."

"In Texas," he said, his eyes narrowing. "Why didn't you sleep with him?"

I dropped my face to his chest with a groan. "Why are we talking about this? We were talking about you."

"This *is* about me. Now answer the damn question."

"Your anger is ruining this!" I was appalled at how close I'd come to admitting I loved him, but then he had to go and remind me why I shouldn't love him at all.

"And you're inability to answer a simple question is making me jealous as fuck. I can't stand the thought of you feeling *anything* for him. Now tell me! Why did you send him away?" He paused. "Or maybe you didn't." The timbre of his words grew deadly.

"Gage," I said, grabbing his face, "I *didn't* sleep with him."

"But you wanted to. You've always wanted him, so why didn't you fuck him?"

"Because he deserved better!"

"*He* deserved better?" He shoved me off and jumped from bed. "Better than you? Is that what you think? Perfect Ian Kaplan, golden boy of the century, can do no wrong, right?" The tall, rigid outline of his body towered over me, and I shrank away. "I've got news for you. He doesn't deserve to breathe your name. He knocked up Liz. She was six weeks pregnant when he killed her. I can't even think about it because it makes me so fucking mad I want to tear something apart!"

I blinked, only now aware of the tears streaming down my face. "Gage…"

"I saw you years ago, you know," he said, his tone eerily calm. "During a rare visit when he and I pretended to *fix* things. You were so entranced by him that I wasn't even a blip on your radar." He paused, and the disquiet rang through the room so loudly, I was tempted to cover my ears. "He never got over you, and me destroying you would've destroyed him, but you fucking destroyed me instead. You gave me a glimpse of something I thought I wasn't allowed to have. Fuck, Kayla, neither one of us deserves you." He pulled on a pair of pants and then stomped toward the door.

"Where are you going?"

"Away, before I do something else unforgivable." The door slammed in his wake, and his steps thundered down the hall. I was amazed the disturbance didn't wake Eve.

I sat in bed for a few moments, too stunned to comprehend what had just happened. Before I thought twice about it, I scrambled to my feet, wrapped myself in his satin sheet, and went after him.

It was probably a dumbass move, but I wasn't known for my rational decisions lately. I found him in the hall, his face against the wall, hands fisted at his ears. I tiptoed to his side. Complete darkness blanketed us, and the house was so still it unsettled me. *Gage* was too still.

"How did you know the baby was his?" I was poking an angry tiger with that question, but I didn't care—not if making him mad would get him to open up.

"You really want to do this?" He kept his voice low, probably so he didn't wake Eve.

I let out a breath. "Yes. You can punish me all you want, hurt me if you need to, but I'm not dropping this. You demand all of me? Well I'm demanding all of you. Tell me everything."

He didn't move, didn't look at me, and at first I thought he was going to flat out ignore me. "I can still smell her blood, and maybe it's on my hands as much as his because I went after them that night. I knew she'd been with someone else, but when I found them together...I just lost it." He tightened his fists further, as if he could squeeze the memory into nothing. "She died in my fucking arms, took everything good about me with her, and he never even knew about the baby."

I needed to touch him, possibly more than I'd ever needed to touch another man before. Tentatively, I smoothed my hand over his back, but he sprang out of reach.

"You want to know why I hurt you? I did it because I couldn't let go. It was all I saw at first. Him with his hands on her, and her blood all over mine."

"Gage…I'm…" I gulped, my eyes stinging.

"Go back to bed, Kayla."

"No."

He pounded a fist on the wall. "I could lock you in the basement for the night."

"Do it." God, why couldn't he open up to me? Why was getting him to tell me *anything* like prying a bone from a rabid pit bull?

He moved fast, like a snake striking unsuspecting prey, and hauled me into his arms. The sheet slid from my body, forgotten on the floor as his mouth crushed mine. His kiss silenced my protests as he carried me down the hall, thankfully in the opposite direction of the basement. He kicked the bedroom door shut behind us and threw me onto the bed, and his body followed. I became prisoner to his arms and legs as he slammed into me, his thrusts brutal while his mouth kept mine busy.

Unlike earlier, this was fucking in its basest form.

I couldn't ask questions if he was screwing me like an animal. Logical thought fragmented, leaving me with scattered pieces of the things I needed him to tell me. Ian, Liz, baby, death…Gage's brokenness. I'd never noticed that about him before. Thought I was the only broken one, and he was just the fucked up one.

Focus. What were we talking…no, arguing about?

My body betrayed me, and I stopped caring about anything other than the feel of him moving inside me. I came with a breathless cry, my hands fisting the pillows as I arched into him. This had to be a record. I'd never had so many orgasms in one night.

And I never wanted it to end.

His groan of release rumbled onto my lips, and in the afterglow of the explosion, he tucked me against him before sleep claimed us.

11. HESITANT

Neither of us mentioned our argument, but it colored every word we spoke, every movement we made within that house. Gage worked from home in order to keep an eye on me, but also because his business wasn't the same since he'd gone to prison. Most of his clients had taken their accounts elsewhere, and he'd worked his ass off to regain the trust of the loyal few who stayed with him. I found it surprising he had any clients left after the scandal, but that was Gage; he inspired loyalty even when he didn't deserve it.

And that was the cause of my hesitation now. I gripped Eve's tiny hand in mine and pressed a finger to my mouth.

"Are we playing a game?" she whispered.

"Shh." I nodded and pulled her toward the front door. Gage's muffled voice drifted from behind the ajar door of his office. Agitation tinted his tone, and I imagined him pacing in front of his desk as he spoke into his cell. His distraction was my chance. A few more steps, a quiet turn of the knob, and Eve and I would be free. I'd find the nearest house and use the phone to call the police.

So why was I hesitating?

The past week replayed in my mind. Despite the tension between us, I'd seen yet a different side of him. Just yesterday, he'd taught Eve how to tie her shoes, which was amazing considering she was only four. He'd already won her over, and I knew she'd miss him when we left.

I couldn't stay though, no matter how much part of me wanted to—how much I was tempted to risk everything to be with him. My biggest mistake was allowing him in, because what he'd done was unforgivable. Normal, sane people didn't kidnap the ones they claimed to love. I firmed my resolve and gripped the cold doorknob.

"Don't go," he said softly behind me.

I whirled and found him standing a few feet away. Eve ran to him without hesitation.

"You found us!"

"I did." He grinned as he picked her up. "It's getting late. I'll tuck you in, princess."

She giggled at the nickname and wound her toddler arms around his neck, holding on tight.

I slumped against the door as his gaze pinned me. I couldn't read his expression, which was scarier than shit as it left me not knowing what to expect.

He closed the distance between us and dug a key out of his pocket. "Wait for me in the basement," he said, dropping the key into my hand.

"Is Mommy in trouble?" Eve asked.

"Everything's fine," he assured her, yet I detected something in his tone. Everything was not fine, and I was about to learn about it the hard way.

My body went cold. I hadn't been down there since the day he'd put his ring on my finger. "Gage…"

"Wait for me," he repeated.

Helplessly, I watched him disappear down the hall with Eve, leaving me a shaking mess in his wake. I wanted to run after him and snatch Eve away, but my feet wouldn't work. And who was I kidding anyway? Getting into a physical tug-of-war with him, my daughter the prize, wouldn't end well.

I forced my feet in the direction he'd ordered me, stumbling twice on the way to that closed off dark space. After turning the key in the lock, I swung the door wide and reached for the light switch. Not knowing what he was about to do to me, I undressed and waited for him on my knees, hands behind my back, like I had every night since he'd let me out of the basement. His voice drifted through the monitor as he wished Eve sweet dreams, and a few minutes later, the creak of the door echoed through the space, followed by the click of the lock. His quiet steps brought him downstairs.

"Please don't hurt me."

He strode to where I knelt and glared at me. "I'm not going to hurt you. I thought…" He took a breath and ran a hand down his face. "I thought we'd gotten somewhere this past week, but the second I'm not looking, you try to leave."

"I'm sorry," I said.

"Are you?" He threw a key onto the floor and stepped back. "Go. If you want to leave me so badly, then take Eve and go. I won't stop you."

Why wasn't I moving? I imagined my fingers clasping the key, saw myself dress and climb the stairs. Even heard the door opening. Felt Eve in my arms as we escaped into the cold. We'd go back to Texas and life would go back to the way it'd been before he showed up in my driveway. I'd work, Eve would go to daycare after preschool let out, and we'd spend our Saturdays with Stacey and her son. It was a good life.

"Why aren't you going?"

"I don't know."

"Yes you do. Stop lying to me, but more importantly, stop lying to yourself."

"I…I want you."

"You've always wanted me, Kayla. That's not why you aren't running right now." He unbuckled his belt, and I stiffened as he pulled it from his pant loops. "If you stay, I'm going to punish you, but you're not staying unless you tell me why."

"You'll make me leave?"

"Yes."

I squeezed my eyes shut and forced the words from my lips. "I love you."

His breath hitched. "Was that so hard to admit?"

More than he'd ever know. "I shouldn't love you."

"We all do things we shouldn't." He pulled me to my

feet. "Get on the bench."

My body betrayed me again. Even though I shook with fear, desire bloomed low in my belly. I crawled onto the spanking bench and draped it like a rag doll as he strapped me down. He raised my ass, but instead of striking me, he palmed my bottom, both hands kneading flesh. His fingers teased the hole I knew he wanted to penetrate again.

"We only said anal sex was off the table. We didn't talk about anal play."

I moaned. The thought did funny things to me.

"Is that a yes?"

"Mmm-hmm." I swallowed hard as tingles shot down my thighs.

The chilly air stirred as he moved away. He returned moments later, and his fingers drew lazy circles around the opening of that forbidden place. I hissed in a breath when he inserted a finger.

"Do you like that?"

Unable to form words, I mumbled a yes.

"I'm going to make your ass red. Do you want my hand or my belt?"

"Your hand."

"Count them out loud. I won't stop until you tell me to."

What was he doing? Why was he giving me control of my punishment? I didn't have time to question him. His palm came down hard.

"One," I moaned, and he struck again. I gasped at the force and squeaked out, "Two."

Each strike grew in power, yet I kept counting. It didn't occur to me to say stop. Not when I was liquefying between my thighs despite the tears sliding down my cheeks, dripping off my chin to the floor.

With every strike of his palm, he brought out guttural cries, similar to the sounds I'd made during labor, but he didn't ease up, and he didn't order me into silence either.

"Fifty," I sobbed.

"Tell me to stop."

The word stuck in my throat, refused to form on my tongue. Instead, I kept counting.

And he kept spanking. Harder—so hard I was certain my ass would be one huge bruise after this.

"Fifty-eight!" I yelled, hands clenched in the restraints.

"Damn it, Kayla! Say stop!"

"Stop!"

He dropped his head onto my back, and his five o'clock shadow chafed my skin like sandpaper. I felt his heavy breaths puff across my burning ass. "Why didn't you tell me to stop?"

"I don't know." My body shut down, and I had nothing left in me, no more fighting power. I couldn't even gather my thoughts. Nothing made sense. I closed my eyes and wished for sleep.

"Yes, you do. Tell me why."

"Because I shouldn't want you. I shouldn't want this."

"But you do."

"Yes." I let out a cry, a cross between a sob and a hiccup. "What kind of person does that make me? What kind of mother?"

"What we do in the privacy of our bedroom or down here has nothing to do with your parenting. You're an incredible mother. Eve will grow up strong. Don't ever doubt that." He smoothed a palm over my bottom, and I gasped as pain radiated from where he touched. "You are the most sexy woman alive, especially when I mark you like this. God, baby. You have no idea what you do to me." He spread my wetness to my ass before slowly inserting a finger.

I groaned. "Are you trying to make me beg for it?"

"I don't need to try. I have no doubt you'll beg me to take you anally." He removed his finger and nudged me with the cool tip of a butt plug. I held my breath, enduring first the pressure then the burn as he shoved it all the way in. "But not tonight. Tonight you're being punished."

"Thought you already punished me."

"That wasn't punishment."

"It wasn't?"

He laughed. "Hardly. You wanted it too much."

"What are you gonna do then?" Fear snuck into my tone. Damn. Fear always got him going.

"How turned on are you?" He slid his other hand between my thighs.

"Oh…" Moaning, I rubbed myself against his fingers. "Very." I wanted him so badly, I could crawl inside him and it still wouldn't be enough.

"Good. That's your punishment. I'll keep you aroused to the breaking point all night, but you won't get off. It'll serve as a reminder that leaving me will leave you sexually frustrated for the rest of your life."

"You're evil."

He released my ankles and wrists. "But you love me, so I couldn't be that bad." His words reeked of satisfaction. "Come on," he said, helping me to my feet. "Let's move this to our bedroom. We might as well get comfortable, since you have a long night of punishment ahead of you."

12. DENIED

This was the most wicked form of punishment ever. He'd restrained me to the bed, and I couldn't move.

At all.

Rope bound my skin in a soft texture, and my knees were bent and spread wide. He'd tied my ankles to my thighs and had extended the rope to the bed posts to keep me that way. My arms were stretched above and fastened to the headboard. He had me exactly where he wanted me—helpless and at his mercy, which was nonexistent.

He licked a slow path down my center, dipped into my entrance, and then glided his tongue to the aching bud of nerves he knew would break me if he put the right amount of pressure there. He'd been at this for the last forty-five minutes, according to the clock on the nightstand.

"You're so fucking wet. I bet you want to come so bad right now."

My only answer was a whimper. I'd clamped my lips

closed since he'd started his torture methods. Why add to his pleasure with verbal confirmation his punishment was working?

"You're much too quiet." He turned around and eased his cock between my lips, and his tongue went back to work between my thighs.

I whimpered again as he pushed deeper into my mouth. The taste of him speared through me, and I felt warmth flood under his lips and tongue. An unrestrained moan vibrated around his cock. I was so close.

"Too close, baby," he said, ceasing his erotic kiss. "You're not coming tonight." He blew a cool breath over inflamed, heated flesh, making my insides clench. I squirmed in desperation. His hips bucked, and he deepened his possession of my mouth, hitting the back of my throat. My heart raced in fear.

Don't gag, don't gag, I told myself.

He came with a hoarse cry, and I was so hot with need I would have begged without shame, but I was too busy swallowing. He pulled from my mouth and knelt between my legs again, where he rubbed me to insanity.

I squeezed my eyes shut as involuntary sounds rumbled from my lips. "Please let me come," I said sometime later, for the fifth...no, sixth or seventh time. My hips rocked constantly, though I couldn't seem to bring myself closer to the hand causing so much pleasure and frustration simultaneously. "Please. I can't take it. Fuck me anally if you want...please..."

"No."

Why was I being punished again?

I must have asked the question out loud, because he answered, "You tried leaving without permission."

I drew in a shuddering breath as more pressure built. "You'll let me out of the house with permission?"

"Eventually, yes, when I can trust you not to bolt." His lips curved into a smile. "After tonight, the way you stayed, even admitted you loved me so you could stay, I think we're reaching that point."

Conversation distracted me from the ache he refused to relieve, so I kept talking. "If I asked to go to the mall for lunch or a coffee, you'd let me?"

"It would depend." He leaned down and added his tongue for a few strokes.

"God! Gage…" *Focus.* "Depend on what?"

He looked up from between my thighs, a sheen of my desire on his lips. "On whether you'd earn that privilege. I told you there'd be rules that govern your behavior, and I meant it. You'll be allowed friends—*female* friends—but only if I approve of them first."

"You're planning to control every aspect of my life?" Was he serious?

"Yes," he said simply. "I control your orgasms"—he pressed hard on my clit, making me shake—"your schedule, your relationships with others." He paused, growing even more serious. "I'm a jealous man, Kayla. That hasn't changed. You'll never be allowed to talk to other men in a casual or social setting. Your words are for me only, your ideas and dreams are mine. This body is mine."

"Am I supposed to ignore every man on the planet?

Even to the point of rudeness?"

"No. You speak to other men only when necessary, and you excuse yourself when it isn't." He gave me a stern look. "And it is *never* necessary for you to see or talk to my brother. I want him out of your life for good."

I was pretty sure that wouldn't be a problem after our last encounter. Gage had allowed me to return Stacey's frantic calls, and I'd discreetly checked my call log. Ian hadn't tried to contact me once.

"This sounds like a lot," he said, "but you'll adjust. I do want you to have friends and interests outside of me, but that doesn't happen until they go by me first, understand?"

Oh, I understood all right, and his tone was pissing me off.

"What if I decide to leave? Will you let me?"

He crawled up my body until we were face to face, and his intoxicating breath mingled with mine. "You can leave, but you'll never be allowed back. Ever. Leave me, and it'll be for good."

He'd given me my freedom, so why wasn't I jumping for it?

Because you love him, you dumbass, and he knows it. He knows you're not going anywhere.

"The good news about these rules," he continued, "is that Eve will follow them too when she's older. No boyfriends until she's sixteen, and they'll have to pass our inspection, as will her friends. I'm sure you can agree with me on this point."

He was right. I did agree, but I still didn't appreciate

being treated the same way.

"I'm an adult, Gage. These 'rules' of yours leave no foundation for trust. You don't trust me, and you never will. You take and take and take, but you give nothing in return."

He was too quiet, and I wasn't sure if he was going to blow a fuse or ignore the issue entirely. "You're right," he said.

That was the last thing I expected him to say. "I am?"

"I have a hard time trusting. I'm working on it."

"Well…you've been working on compromising too, so why don't we go back to that?"

"Such as?" he asked.

"I won't flirt with men. I have no interest to anyway since I'm so hung up on you." I rolled my eyes. "God help me. I don't know why, but I am." A huge grin spread across his face. "But you need to trust me," I continued. "Just because I talk to some random guy at the coffee shop about the latest song or movie doesn't mean anything. It's called polite chatter, and people do it all the time."

He shook his head. "No. *You* don't. *You* belong to me and only me. If you have something to say about music or movies, you come to me. You don't seem to get it, Kayla. I want every part of you, and your behavior will honor that. If this hypothetical coffee shop guy asks you what you think of the new Britney Spears song, you say, 'thanks for the coffee, but I have to go,' and you fucking walk away." He gripped my chin so I had no choice but to look at him. "Do you understand me?"

"I understand," I mumbled.

"You're *mine*, and I won't compromise on this. If you want to leave the house, you ask for permission first. I'll expect a rundown on where you're going, who with, what you're doing, and when you'll be back—and you'd better be back in time or face punishment."

It was all I could do not to sneer at him. "So basically I *am* a child then."

He smirked. "Your tone right now suggests it, but no. You're simply mine, and you'll do as I say."

He reached behind him and produced a gag. "Now enough of this. If you're still able to form coherent sentences, then I haven't been doing my job." He glanced at the clock. "You have at least three more hours of writhing on this bed before I let you sleep."

He pushed the gag into my mouth before continuing with his torture methods. My eyes rolled back after he started in with a vibrator. Guantanamo Bay had nothing on Gage Channing.

13. CRAZY NORMAL

"Mommy, are you awake?"

The whisper awoke me. I rubbed sleep from my eyes and found my daughter standing next to the bed. The wafting smell of something delicious drifted into the bedroom, and I sat up, realizing that Gage had freed my hands. He'd worked me into a frenzied state last night, and no amount of my muffled begging had changed his mind. He'd punished me all right. I still ached, still wanted him badly, but he'd made sure my hands were tied out of reach for the rest of the night. The binding had been loose enough to sleep comfortably but had left me incapable of reaching the aching spot between my thighs.

"I'm not 'spose to wake you up," Eve said, breaking through my thoughts. "How come you didn't sleep enough? Gage says you need sleep."

I ruffled her hair. "What's he doing?"

"Cooking French toast." She furrowed her brows. "How does the toast get Frenched?"

My mouth quirked as I peeked underneath the

comforter to find my body nestled in one of his shirts. I must have been out cold if he'd dressed me without rousing me from sleep. "Come here," I said with a smile. "You silly girl." I opened my arms so she could pounce into them.

"I like our new house," she said as her arms tightened around me. "He's nice."

Her blind trust seared my heart. I glanced at the ring on my finger and gulped. Could I really go through with the wedding? He'd given us our freedom. I could leave anytime with Eve, and he said he wouldn't stop me.

But could I walk away from him? Each day we spent together, each small change I saw in him, slowly erased what he'd put me through last year. Something about him was different. The sadism was still there, the need for power and control still an innate part of him, but I'd also witnessed slivers of compassion and humanity.

Which one was the real Gage Channing? The cold, out-of-control sadistic man who'd whipped me until welts covered my body? The man who'd fucked me in front of his own brother for revenge? Or the man who'd won over my daughter? The man who was trying to take into consideration my needs and wants.

The man who said he loved me.

I closed my eyes, and my lungs expanded as I breathed deep. I felt so much with him—too much—and I couldn't imagine never feeling this way again.

"What's the matter?" Eve asked, her palms holding my cheeks. "Are you sick?"

"No, I'm fine." I flung the covers back. "Come on,

let's go check on breakfast." We padded into the hall, and I was glad his shirt fell past my thighs since I wasn't wearing any panties.

The sweet aroma of breakfast wreaked havoc with my senses and my stomach. God, it smelled good. My belly rumbled, and I couldn't recall being so hungry in a long time.

"Good morning." He smiled at Eve as she hopped to his side. "Why don't you get to work on that picture you wanted to color for your mom? I got the art supplies down for you, princess."

"Okay!" She didn't walk—she ran down the hall toward her bedroom.

I narrowed my eyes. "You're trusting a four-year-old with crayons, unsupervised?"

"You worry too much. Let her have fun. They're washable anyway." He gestured for me to join him. The instant I got within reach, he turned me so my back faced him and pushed me against the counter. The plate of French toast teased my nose, sitting only a few inches away, and my stomach rumbled again.

His hands slipped underneath my shirt—his shirt—and he palmed my breasts. "You look so fucking sexy in my shirt. If Eve weren't in the other room, I'd fuck you right here on the counter." He nudged my bottom with his hard-on. "I like you bare-assed. From now on, you're not allowed to wear underwear. I want access at all times."

I groaned.

"Last night, you begged. I've been very patient, Kayla, but no more. This ass is mine."

Nearly breathless, I let my head fall back on his shoulder. "What you did last night was not fair."

"It was more than fair. You'll never escape punishment. Some will be easier to take than others, but I'll always punish you when you disobey me." He flicked my nipples, making me flinch.

"Does it hurt?" he asked, his voice husky at my ear.

"Mmm-hmm." My nipples were incredibly sensitive, and my breasts seemed heavier than usual in his hands.

"Good. That means you're still aroused."

Footsteps sounded in the hall, and Gage stepped away from me. "You have an appointment after breakfast, by the way."

"What?" I asked, freezing to the spot as Eve bounded to me, picture in hand. Numbly, I took the drawing and stared at the colors. A rainbow. A ray of hope in a grey sky. How symbolic. But rainbows were rare, and I'd yet to find a pot of gold at the end of one.

"What appointment?"

"The seamstress. She needs to measure you for your gown. She'll have designs for you to go through too. Pick any one you want. Don't worry about the cost." He picked up the plate of French toast and moved toward the table as if he hadn't just dropped a bomb on me. Eve followed on his heels. She liked to shadow him whenever possible.

I'm not ready for this, I thought as the two of them moved around the table, arranging plates and flatware. Eve beamed as she helped. I stood in a daze, my pulse pounding in my ears, and he had to ask me twice to join them.

"Gage…" I swallowed hard and pushed the food around my plate. A few minutes ago I'd been starving; now the thought of food made me want to retch. Would he go ballistic if I said I didn't want to rush this? My eyes fell on Eve, who remained unaware of the tension spiraling out of control in my stomach.

"What is it, Kayla?"

I glanced up and met his indigo eyes. They always deepened to that color when he was angry. Obviously, I was transparent to him. "Nothing." I pushed my toast to one side of the plate, then flipped the pieces over to the other.

"Say what's on your mind." He measured his tone, no doubt because a four-year-old witnessed our conversation, but I didn't miss the edge to his words.

"It's happening so fast."

"As it should. I know what I want, Kayla, and it's going to happen."

"What's gonna happen?" Eve asked.

I sighed, and Gage shook his head. "You and your mom are going out today. Maybe she'll take you for ice cream after lunch."

Eve grinned. "Can we have the rainbow kind?"

"Sure, baby," I said.

We finished breakfast in silence. Afterward, I retreated to the bathroom to shower. Gage checked on me several times to make sure I wasn't finishing what he'd started the night before. He'd made the rules perfectly clear, just as they'd been a year ago.

No masturbating.

He sat on the bed as I dressed, and his gaze never strayed. "Your purse is in the closet by the door. I'll have to unlock it for you. The keys to the Lexus are in there. I also gave you a credit card—use it for whatever you want. It's yours."

I dropped the ankle-length skirt I'd just pulled from the closet—the one he'd stocked with an unimaginable amount of clothing in my size four. It chilled me to realize the extent he'd gone to in order to get me here under his control.

"I'm not taking your money. I'm capable of making my own."

"Bullshit. Eve needs you home more than you need to work. That's a discussion that won't happen until she's in school full days."

I took a deep breath to sooth the anger roiling through me. "Gage, I'm not taking—"

"My money *is* your money. You're going to be my wife soon."

I set my hands on my hips. "How soon?"

"Three weeks."

My knees grew weak. "It's…that's too soon!"

"No, it's not."

How could he remain so calm? I was about to fall apart, and he just sat there, the perfect picture of relaxed. It was disturbing…and infuriating! I clenched my hands. "What if I say no?"

He rose from the bed. Eve's voice blasted through the monitor, and I jumped before realizing she was only playing. Gage moved toward me, a predatory glint in his eyes.

"You won't."

"You seem sure of yourself."

"I am." He grasped my head in both hands, not quite forcefully but not gently either. "I'm one hundred percent certain you'll meet me at the altar in three weeks, as I'm positive you'll be back tonight in time for dinner."

"How can you be so sure?" I whispered, my throat thickening because I sure as hell wasn't sure.

His lips quirked into a satisfied smile. "You're addicted to me. You were a year ago, and you're more so now. I'll never get the image of you last night out of my head. You were the definition of a wild animal, Kayla, reduced to your most basic desires and needs. You will always come back to me."

His mouth lowered to mine, demanded I let him in, and I did. I always did. He kissed me until I was breathless, until I couldn't remember what we'd been talking about, and I kissed him back just as greedily. I was lucky I still remembered my own name.

His hands slid from my cheeks, and I watched, in a trance, as he disappeared into the hall.

14. DOUBT

I had a major problem, thanks to Gage's new rule that I wasn't allowed to wear panties. I had to face the seamstress without any. She was gracious enough not to say anything, but it was just one more bit of humiliation at the hands of my future husband.

Husband.

That word stirred all kinds of feelings in me—all of them contradictory in nature. So I went through the motions, picked out a gorgeous dress that dipped low at the bust and sparkled with intricate artistry, and I smiled like a woman facing the best day of her life. The gown was designed to hug a woman's curves before flowing to the floor in satin and lace. If I was going to walk down the aisle, at least Gage would drool like a dog as I put one foot in front of the other. I even pretended the price tag didn't matter.

Though it did. Everything mattered, but what mattered to me didn't matter to him. I drove his car, spent his money, and took Eve out for lunch and ice cream. I even bought her a new princess Barbie because that was her new obsession since he'd handed her everything she'd ever want on a silver platter.

Time didn't understand my trepidation; it moved too swiftly and now the big day was only a week away. My stomach was in constant knots from the stress, and I could barely eat, despite Gage demanding I do so. Apparently, he liked my curves and expected me to eat enough so I wouldn't turn into a skeleton of myself. He'd already taken his belt to me twice over the issue, and God, those lashes had left their mark.

But the thought of food sickened me. Marrying him…I didn't know how to feel about it. I couldn't bring myself to leave him, but I didn't know if I could say "I do" either. Marriage was a big step—a bigger step than any conventional couple faced. Saying "I do" to Gage meant I would wait for him on my knees every night. I'd have no independence, no freedom. He would always hold my free will in his fist, and the difference between sleeping at his side or being locked in the basement lay in my ability to bend to his rules and demands.

He wielded his authority over me more powerfully than a parent did a child, yet he also loved me—loved me with single-minded focus and an intense need to own every part of me. His love was selfish and obsessive but also unconditional in a most conditional way. I couldn't even explain what that meant, but my heart understood. His love was sick and tainted and all wrong, but it was mine. He stood at the epicenter of my world, cast it in crimson, and I was ashamed to admit I rather liked living in red.

I *was* addicted to him.

"Mommy?"

I snapped to attention and found Eve's inquisitive eyes on me. We sat in the middle of the busy food court at the mall. Gage and I had met with the wedding planner earlier for a cake tasting appointment, and he'd gone to Channing Enterprises afterward to attend to some business. He was starting to trust me on my own, which said a lot. I'd promised to eat something, but I was beginning to think Chinese was a poor choice. The little I'd eaten sat lodged in my throat, holding the panic down so it couldn't bubble over.

I'm marrying Gage Channing in a week.

Only a week.

Seven days.

Am I crazy?

Stupid question.

Eve called to me again from across the tiny table. She'd refused to sit at my side in a booster seat. She was a *big girl* now. I shook my head and focused my attention on her. "Yeah, baby?"

"Can we come here for one hundred days?" She wrinkled her nose. "But not for Chinese!"

I forced a smile because I doubted Gage would let me bring her to the mall on a regular basis. "Maybe we can do this once a week. I'll have to ask…" I cut off, horrified by what I'd almost said. I did not want my daughter growing up thinking it was normal to ask a man for permission to do something as simple as leave the house.

Relationships were supposed to be give-and-take—a partnership. Just because I'd become entrapped didn't mean she had to.

"You ready to go, princess?" I stalled, the nickname hanging in the air. When had I started using his nickname for my daughter? Acid burned my throat, and I swallowed hard. Suddenly, the urge to go home and fall into bed overwhelmed me.

When had I started thinking of his place as home?

Too many questions, and I had no answers. I was too drained to hunt for them. I disposed of our trash from lunch, and Eve and I window-shopped on the way to the mall's exit. She was a typical four-year-old who wanted everything her gaze touched.

"*Please?*" she whined.

"Not today," I said. She was about to argue, but the blonde entering the mall caught her attention.

"Mommy, look!"

I followed the direction Eve pointed, and my heart dropped. Katherine. Please, anyone but her.

Fate wasn't listening. She faltered at the site of us, and Eve squealed an excited greeting. I clenched my teeth, hating that my daughter liked the woman. Katherine's lips curved into a wicked smile as she sauntered toward us.

"Well isn't this a coincidence? How's Gage?" she asked, though her tone hinted at hostility.

"He's fine," I snapped. "How's your son? Everything work out for you in court?"

It was official; Gage Channing had turned me into a territorial bitch.

Her nasty grin vanished. "That's none of your business."

I brushed my bangs back with my left hand, purposefully flaunting the large diamond. "Well, we need to get home. Nice chatting with you."

She pursed her lips, her eyes narrowing as she stared at the ring. "Drive safe. The weather's horrid." She smiled at Eve, and as she brushed by, she leaned toward me, her mouth inches from my ear. "Just so you know," she said, lowering her voice, "Gage fucked me while you were down in the basement. He's better at it than his brother, isn't he?"

A deep chill traveled the length of my body, and I absently heard Eve call out "bye" to Katherine. My mind went numb, and the cold barely penetrated as we left the mall and found Gage's Lexus. Eve talked the whole way home, but my head was somewhere else.

I was still standing in the middle of the busy mall, hearing those words that knifed through my heart.

When we arrived back at the house, Eve barreled through the door in search of Gage. I figured he'd still be at work, so I was surprised when he appeared from his office. He picked her up, and as she chattered about our day, about the movie we saw and how she tried "yucky noodles" at the food court, his gaze roamed over me.

He let her slide to her feet. "I need a moment with your mom. You left the puzzles out from this morning. Go put them away, please."

At least he was polite when he demanded things of my daughter. She looked less than thrilled, but she wandered down the hall, swinging her arms and taking her time.

Gage crossed the space between us. "What's wrong?"

I opened my mouth but nothing came out.

"Kayla," he warned. "Answer me."

I wasn't sure what came over me, but my palm shot out and connected with his cheek. My eyes burned with unshed tears, and I moved to strike him again. He grabbed my wrist and squeezed.

"What the hell do you think you're doing?"

I blinked, and the tears spilled. "I ran into Katherine. She said you slept with her."

His eyes narrowed. "You already know about my past with her. I've never kept that a secret."

"I'm not talking about the past. You had me locked in the basement, keeping me from my own child, and you couldn't keep it in your pants for a day?"

"Is that what she told you?" He let go of my wrist.

"Yes."

"She lied. She wanted to, even embarrassed herself trying, but I didn't touch her." He grabbed my hands and held them at my back, and his arms imprisoned my body. "I'm not a cheating bastard, Kayla."

"You let her suck your cock in your office a year ago." Hearing their moans through the door hadn't bothered me at the time, but the memory of that trashy encounter now took my breath. My chest ached from holding back the hurt.

"A year ago, we weren't engaged." He let go of my hands and framed my cheeks, his thumbs wiping away tears. "A year ago, I wasn't in love with you." His voice grew stern. "Your jealousy is a major turn-on, but don't you *ever* hit me again." He glanced at his watch and then folded my fingers around a key. "Go to the basement and pick a corner. Face it, on your knees. I'll punish you once Eve goes down for her nap."

I nodded, my throat too constricted to speak. He took off down the hall toward Eve's room, and I headed for the basement. I removed my clothing and dropped to my knees in the far corner of the rectangular room. The flood of tears wouldn't stop, and as time passed, I wondered why I was still crying. I believed him. I wasn't sure how or why, but Katherine's claim rang false in my heart. So why was I such a mess over this? The thought of him with anyone else brought out my claws, and suddenly, I understood Gage a little better.

My knees were on fire when the door to the basement opened.

"Get up, Kayla."

I rose, rubbing my aching knees as I stood, and turned to face him. He grabbed a paddle from his collection, pulled a chair into the middle of the room, and sat down. "Come here."

I shook my head. "No paddles."

"I said no bullwhip. My belt and hand turn you on too much, and you need to be punished. This is going to hurt. Now get over here."

Wiping my eyes, I walked to him and forced down the pain that consumed me from the inside. He draped me over his lap, his thighs heating my abs as I tipped forward.

I braced myself with both palms on the floor and teetered, feet in the air. He curled his fingers around my side and brought me against his waist.

"You understand why you're being punished so severely, right?"

"Because I hit you."

"That's part of it, yes, but you failed to trust me. You let someone else's lies cloud your judgment. I own you, Kayla. Don't you understand that you own me as well?" Goose bumps broke out on my skin, and the delicious chill spread when he squeezed my ass. "You're mine, and I'm yours, and no one is coming between that." He settled his hand at my side again. "If you get wet, I won't let you come."

Shit. I was already turned on. When had this happened? When had being spanked and humiliated gone from scary to arousing? His return to my life had done something to me, as if he'd come back and flipped the switch he'd installed a year ago but hadn't tripped. Until now.

The paddle came down in quick succession, and I lost count as I howled. He put a lot of strength into those strikes, probably more than he ever had. I squirmed with each one, but still, moisture collected between my thighs. He'd discovered a new form of punishment—one that gave him exactly what he wanted. I couldn't help my body's response, and he knew it. Just like a couple of weeks ago, he'd deny me again.

"No one is coming between us. Do you understand me, Kayla? Not Ian, not Katherine, *no one*."

"But Katherine wants to. Why?" I asked. "What's your history with her?"

"You want to ask questions?" The paddle hit my ass with two loud smacks. "One for every question."

I hissed in a breath. "I don't care. I want to know."

"We had a casual arrangement for a few months. We fucked a few times a week, and she let me do whatever I wanted. I ended it when she said she loved me."

I squeezed my eyes shut, trying to block out the image of them together, but it refused to vanish from my mind. "Did you bring her down here?"

Another painful smack rent the air.

"Yes."

"Was she better than me?"

The question seemed to catch him off guard for a few moments, and his next strike was especially hard. "That's a stupid question. No one compares to you. Come on, get up." He dropped the paddle and helped me to my feet. "Spread your legs." I did as told, and he slid his fingers into my drenched opening. "You are so busted," he said with a smirk. He unzipped his pants and freed his erection.

Our eyes met and held, and I knew he'd make me pay. He reached out, spun me around, and pulled me onto his lap so I sat astride but facing away. Grabbing my hips, he forced my body up and down his shaft, and I couldn't control my moans.

"I own you," he said as he pushed deeper. "Say it."

"You own me."

His fingers dug into my hipbones. "I want to hear you

say it, Kayla."

"You own me, Master." I groaned as he hit my spot—
the spot.

I was going to come.

He pulled me flush against him, cock buried deep,
and went still. "You don't have permission."

"I can't help it, Gage. You feel so good."

"So do you," he murmured. "But you're not coming.
If you can't control yourself, then suck me off."

Resigned, I got to my knees and obeyed.

15. O.M.G.

I dreaded this day, possibly more than my approaching wedding day.

Eve was going back to preschool.

"Are you excited, baby?" I asked her.

With a nod, she picked at her breakfast.

"Nervous?" Gage used his fork to spear an untouched piece of sausage from her plate and brought it to her mouth. "Try it." She took the bite and chewed slowly. "So what do you think?" he asked.

"Good."

"So is preschool. You'll make friends and learn things. Before long, you'll be the smartest one in this house."

She giggled. "Will not! I'm only four." Her face grew serious. "I don't wanna leave."

"Why not?" I asked.

"What if the teacher isn't as nice as Ms. Barns? What if I miss you?"

Her words impacted me like a punch to the gut. I hated the thought of her going back to school, but I had to put my selfish feelings aside. "Everyone will love you, and you'll have so much fun you won't have time to miss me. I promise."

After breakfast, I got Eve ready, and we waited by the front door for the bus to pull up. Gage watched as he loaded the dishwasher. He demonstrated an oddly domestic affinity in the kitchen. Rain fell outside, hitting the roof in a calming staccato beat, and drops of water squiggled down the window.

"Bus is here," I said.

Eve gripped my hand. "Do I have to go?"

I crouched in front of her. "Remember how much fun you had in Texas?"

She nodded.

"See? You'll do great, and I'll be here waiting when you get back." I settled her Dora backpack onto her shoulders, adjusted her coat, and pulled the door open. We jogged through the downpour. Eve forced a smile, the picture of brave as she climbed those steps. The bus driver greeted her as I stood back, my eyes stinging as I folded my arms to ward off the chill. I watched the bus disappear around the corner before returning indoors, and without warning, tears erupted.

Gage gathered me in his arms and just held me. The gesture was so sweet, so unlike him, that I clung to his body and soaked up every second. His embraced tightened, eliciting a sigh from my lips. If he'd hold me like this forever, maybe I'd be okay.

He inched away with a frown. "You don't look good."

"I don't feel good."

He laced his fingers with mine and tugged me toward the hall. "Take a nap. I haven't been letting you get enough sleep."

No, he'd been worshipping my body every night, when he wasn't punishing me.

He stalled at the door to our room and held it open for me. I'd just taken a step toward the bed when nausea rose so swiftly, I knew I wouldn't make it to the bathroom in time. I sprinted anyway, determined not to make a mess, and slammed to the tile in front of the toilet. Chunks of sausage and eggs flew everywhere, mostly on the floor because I missed.

"I'm sorry," I mumbled after I'd purged the last bit of substance from my stomach.

"What the fuck for? Jeez, Kayla. Get up." He pulled me to my feet and shoved a cool washcloth into my hands. "I'll take care of the mess. Get in bed."

I climbed between the sheets, and a buzzing began in my ears, low at first until the sound grew so loud it made me dizzy. It wasn't actual buzzing—not like what people sometimes experience when they suffer from vertigo. No, this buzzing was a disturbing realization that didn't want to form in my mind.

But it did, and it took me right back to the morning, so many years ago, when I awoke in Ian's arms. I'd spewed chunks all over his floor then too, and later that day I'd stared at two lines while my mouth hung open, as if to catch flies.

No. Impossible. I was on birth control.

Except for Texas.

Oh God.

And we hadn't exactly taken precautions during the seven day waiting period when I first began the birth control pills.

Oh. My. God.

"Gage?" My voice wasn't my own. The high-pitched squeak belonged to some crazed woman who was a thread away from falling into the abyss.

"Just a second. Be right there."

I heard water running and the opening and closing of cupboards before he entered the bedroom. The mattress pressed low where he sat behind me, but I couldn't bring myself to turn and look at him. We'd never talked about kids. More kids, that was. He was patient and kind with Eve, more so than I ever imagined, but to add more children to this insane situation...well, *that* would be insane.

But I was getting ahead of myself. I was sick from a bug or bad food or side effects from being on the pill.

He settled his palm on my arm. "What can I do?"

Why did he keep showing parts of himself that made me love him more? I couldn't keep up with his personality shifts. "I think...I mean..."

"Just spit it out, Kayla."

"I'm worried I'm...pregnant." I peeked at him but saw no reaction on his face.

"You're not pregnant. It's likely a bug, or you're upset because today is Eve's first day back to school."

I pushed into a sitting position. "Regardless, I'll feel better knowing I'm not." I raised my gaze to his, not certain what I'd find, but his expression remained unreadable. "Will you get me a test?"

He opened his mouth, as if to say something, but shook his head instead.

"Gage?"

"You're worrying for nothing, but I'll get you a test."

He left the room, and I heard the jingle of keys followed by the slam of the front door. An hour went by, followed by another. I stalked the front entrance, arms wrapped around me as I waited for Eve. Waited for him. Eve's bus beat him back, and I did my best to push my worries to the back of my mind as she jumped down the steps with a huge grin.

"Have a good day?"

She nodded, going on about her new teacher and friends and the new shapes she'd learned. I opened the door, and we escaped into the house, removing our jackets and wiping rain from our faces. Still preoccupied, I settled her at the kitchen table with a snack and returned to my post by the front door.

What was taking him so long?

Twenty minutes later, his car pulled into the driveway, and something was off about him when he stepped into the foyer. His eyes had darkened to indigo again, and I didn't understand what it meant. It was just a test, and he was probably right.

I wasn't pregnant. I *wasn't*.

He pushed the bag into my hands without looking at me.

"You don't want kids, do you?" I whispered. The idea

of never having another child—I wasn't prepared for the pang of regret the thought produced. Part of me wanted another baby someday. *His* baby, as nuts as it was.

"Go take the test. We'll talk about kids another time."

"Why?"

"Just drop it."

That was his go-to phrase when he refused to talk about something. I clutched the bag, my fingers turning white at the knuckles. So that was it. He was against having kids. We were about to get married in less than a week, and he didn't find it necessary to discuss this with me?

I had nothing else to say, so I made my way to our bedroom. He followed, Eve on his heels, and lingered by the door.

"Come on, Eve. Let's give your mom some space," he said before taking her hand and disappearing from sight.

I eyed the bathroom long after they'd left me alone, and eventually, I forced my feet in that direction. What if I *was* pregnant? Would it change how he felt about me? Did the idea of me pregnant with a huge belly repulse him?

I enclosed myself in the luxurious bath, unsure of why I locked the door. I doubted he'd come in. He appeared to want *his* space. My hands trembled as I read the instructions, and finally, I sat on the toilet and took care of business.

Now just the wait.

Time ticked away in my head, a silent countdown that only spanned one hundred and eighty seconds yet seemed like hours. I sucked in a breath; I hadn't realized I'd been holding it for the last minute.

That little stick taunted me from the counter. Just two small steps, a tilt of my head, and I'd have my answer.

Two lines.

The floor dipped. No, that was me dipping to the cold tile, following the motion of my stomach.

But I'm on birth control…

Texas. Fucking Texas. One time and that was about… three weeks ago.

Holy shit. We were having a baby. My gaze veered to the door, and I never wanted to leave through it. Obviously, he didn't want a baby.

Suck it up, Kayla. The sooner you tell him, the sooner we can deal with it.

He was about to be a father because abortion was out of the question.

I got to my feet, turned the knob, and pushed the door open. He sat on the bed, apparently waiting. I expected to find a hint of worry tightening his lips, stiffening his posture, but he appeared unnervingly calm.

"Where's Eve?"

"I put a movie on for her." He rose and took a step toward me. "Feel better now? I told you not to worry about…" Something in my expression must have penetrated his nonchalant veneer.

"I'm pregnant."

"The hell you are!" His voice thundered through the room. "Where's the test?" He stormed into the bathroom, and I whirled, hot on his heels. I stood by helplessly as he gaped at the evidence.

Crazy, how two pink lines could change so much.

His gaze swerved to me, dark with something resembling hatred, as if this was my fault…as if he hadn't been there too.

"You lied to me," he growled.

What? Shaking my head, I tried to grasp the meaning of his words. When had I ever lied to him? He coaxed the truth from me effortlessly. Lying to him was about as easy as denying him. Impossible.

"I've never lied to you," I said, digging my hands into my hips. "I have no idea what you're getting at. I understand you're shocked, but we're having a baby, and we need to deal with this."

"No!" He lurched forward and slammed me against the wall. His hands pushed on my shoulders, fingers curling, squeezing, until I was shaking all over. "*You* are having a baby, and I have an idea who the father is." He dropped his arms and slumped as the fight left him. "Because it isn't me."

"How can you…" I swallowed, as if I could force down the hurt. Grasping my chest with both hands, I wished I could keep my heart from fracturing, but I couldn't. "How can you say that?"

"Because I can't have children!" He shouted, his hands balling at his sides. I flattened further against the wall; prayed I could sink right through it. He took one last look at me in disgust and tore out of the bathroom.

16. DESTROYED

How had I ended up on the floor? I couldn't remember anything after he'd stormed out.

Except for pain.

It began in my heart, squeezing so tightly I couldn't breathe, couldn't think. I doubled over as his words took over my thoughts, torturing me with the echo of his contempt, and somehow I slid to the floor. Seemed like hours ago, though it was probably only minutes.

"Mommy?"

I glanced up from the ball I'd created. Eve stood in the doorway, her eyes bright with unshed tears and her lips quivering. I was trembling too. I pushed myself up, wiped my eyes, and reached for her.

"Where's Gage, baby?"

"He left. Why did he slam the door?" She pulled away, and her innocent eyes found mine. "I don't like him anymore. He yelled at you."

"He was mad. He'll get over it and say he's sorry." At least, I hoped he would. The idea of raising another kid on my own made my stomach clench, but maybe that was exactly what I should do. He was too volatile to be reliable. I swallowed a sob. How could he think I'd lie to him?

How could I have let myself fall for him?

I replayed what had just happened; searched for a clue as to what the hell he'd been thinking. His rage had taken over, but I'd never seen him so...unglued. He'd looked at me as if I'd torn him in two. I was pregnant, and he was the father, but he didn't believe me.

Why?

I hadn't been with anyone else, so unless this was a miraculous conception, his little swimmers worked just fine.

Eve's voice pierced the chaos in my head, trying to get my attention. I pulled her tighter against me and buried my nose in the hollow of her shoulder, inhaling the sweet and familiar scent of my daughter. I was supposed to *comfort* her, but she did the comforting.

"Everything's okay," I mumbled. "Sometimes people get mad and they need to leave for a while so they can calm down enough to talk."

"Like when you send me to my room for time-outs?" Eve asked.

"Yeah, like that." For a four-year-old, her wisdom astounded me. And she was much too observant. I couldn't fall apart with her here, and Gage and I couldn't go to bat here either, even though I feared we were about to.

Whatever he thought I'd done...I had to make him

see he was wrong.

I picked myself off the floor, literally, and pulled myself together. Hours passed, but Gage still didn't return. I completed chores, cooked dinner, and played with Eve before tucking her in with a bedtime story. Another hour crept by, but still…no Gage.

He didn't allow me a cell phone. I only had access to one when he allowed it or I left the house. The phone, along with my purse and keys were locked in the closet by the door. I couldn't call him, and I couldn't leave unless I took Eve out of there on foot.

As I paced the living room, growing angrier by the second, I seriously considered it. I could wake her, pack a small bag of essentials, and just disappear. Never look back. But I'd tried that last year and look where it had gotten me. He would always find me…as long as he wanted me, and I wasn't so sure he did anymore.

A key turned in the lock, and I froze, eyes on the front door as it swung open. He stumbled in, swayed, and leaned against the wall as he kicked the door shut. He lifted his head and stared at me.

Stared through me.

"Gage, I—"

"Don't say a fucking word." He kept his tone quiet, though his words still produced a nocuous edge. He pushed away from the wall and came at me, his tall body stumbling closer. I backed away, alarmed by the hatred in his eyes and his obvious drunken state.

The back of my thighs hit the arm of the couch and I toppled over. He followed, trapping me with his body and his seething gaze. The scent of rum wafted between us. I clamped my lips shut and waited.

"You swore up and down you didn't fuck him."

Realization enclosed my heart with an icy grip. He was talking about Ian. "I haven't been with anyone but you. *No one*," I said slowly, enunciating each word in hope the truth would penetrate.

His hands shot out fast, fingers curling around my wrists, tightening to the point of pain. He held them prisoner above my head as his face lowered, his sneering lips an inch from mine. "Do *not* lie to me again."

"I'm not lying." My mouth trembled, and the words barely formed between us, despite the narrow space.

He yanked me to my feet, rough enough to make my head swing back, and I was already pleading as he dragged me toward the basement. "Stop! You're drunk. Don't do this now—"

He clamped a hand over my mouth and nose, muffling not only my words, but my air. Panic rushed up, bringing with it nausea and a flood of memories. I was suffocating...

I blinked and hot tears rolled down my face to pool on his hand. I couldn't breathe! I struggled as he unlocked the door; struggled for air, for escape. He switched on the light as I broke free, and I teetered on the top step as the bottom swayed closer, rushing to meet me though my feet still hadn't left solid ground. My hands flailed but found nothing to save me.

With a cry, I envisioned my body twisted and ruined on the floor—the baby and me dead—as gravity pulled at me with her powerful claws.

Gage grabbed me from behind. Not even gravity could match his strength. He fisted the back of my shirt and propelled me down the stairs before pushing me face first onto the bed.

"Don't fight me, Kayla. Cooperate, and it won't hurt as much."

A sob bubbled up. "What are you gonna do?"

"Punish you," he said as he yanked my shirt over my head. He unclasped my bra and pulled it from underneath me, followed by the rest of my clothing.

"For what? I haven't done anything wrong."

"You fucking lied to me!"

"Don't hurt us," I whimpered.

"Us?" He spat the word. "You think I care about you or that…that…*fucking* mistake?" His voice fractured, and so did my composure. I bawled as he stretched out my arms and legs. He tied me to the bed with forceful efficiency, pulling the bindings so tightly they gouged my skin. I didn't even fight him—I didn't have it in me. His words had delivered the final, fatal blow.

I was dead on the inside. I was nothing. He could beat me until I gushed blood and it couldn't possibly hurt this much.

"I loved you!" he roared. "I told you shit I've never told…" His steps faded away. I twisted my head and watched through my tangled hair as he approach his collection of whips and paddles. He pulled that terrifying coil from the wall and unwound it.

"You promised," I whispered.

"If you can lie, so can I."

"I didn't lie to you! I never slept with your brother."

"Don't call him that." He stormed to the bed and made a cracking sound with his weapon of choice.

My muscles tensed. "Please," I begged. "Don't do it. You said you wouldn't. I trusted you!"

"And I trusted you!"

"The baby's yours, Gage. That's the truth. If you do this—"

Fire streaked across my ass, stealing the breath from me. I fisted my hands and tried to crawl out of reach, but he'd made sure I couldn't. Another strike landed, this time on the back of my thighs, eliciting a grunt. I sobbed his name. "I love you!"

That only seemed to anger him more. He swung that whip across my body again, and I screamed. My fingernails bit into my palms, and I concentrated on that pain, focused on the fire dancing up and down my skin— anything to drown out the unbearable ache within me.

I'd given him all of me, but it wasn't enough. He couldn't see beyond his past, couldn't see beyond his own pain.

"The baby's yours," I whispered with each strike, no longer screaming. No longer able. My voice faded as the count rose, but I grasped one tiny word and let it bleed from my lips. "Red."

His fist loosened and the whip slid to the floor. He followed soundlessly, his knees buckling, and burrowed his head into his hands. His body shook as he mumbled words I couldn't decipher. I swam in and out of consciousness for a while, but he didn't move, didn't stop shaking. Eventually, he got to his feet and headed for the stairs.

"You did it," I said. "You destroyed me. But I'm not his anymore, so I guess that means you destroyed what was yours instead."

His steps faltered, and I thought he was going to say something, but moments later the light went out and the door slammed.

17. BANISHED

The darkness nearly suffocated me. I lay restrained to the bed, overcome by claustrophobia even though I had plenty of space around me. My bottom and thighs burned, and I focused on the pain so nothing else would touch me.

He'd gone back on his promise.

That still touched me. His words and actions hurt far worse than the whip he'd just unleashed on my body. Even drunk and enraged, he'd held back.

I wished he hadn't.

I wished he'd broken my body instead of my spirit. Hot tears soaked the sheet under my cheek, and I didn't recall the exact moment I dozed off, but I had to pee something fierce when I awoke. The blackness closed in more with each passing minute, and I had no idea what time it was or how long I'd slept. I was worried for Eve, especially since the monitor had offered nothing but silence. He must have shut it off. I didn't think he'd hurt her, but he wasn't operating on all cylinders either.

The door creaked open and a sliver of light beamed down the staircase. He switched on the overhead light, and I blinked several times until the sudden brightness no longer blinded me. I watched him stomp down the stairs and come toward me. His eyes were bloodshot, more so than last night, as if he hadn't slept at all. He held a bag and my purse in one hand, and he dropped them both before untying me.

"Don't move yet. I need to check your backside."

"It's fine," I muttered. I got to my hands and knees, turned to face him, but the room spun. Nausea hit me from nowhere. I shoved past him, sprinting to the bathroom, and my fingers gripped cool porcelain as I retched into the toilet. After the last dry heave, I flushed away the ugly brown and then relieved my screaming bladder before rinsing the vomit from my mouth.

He hadn't moved at all when I returned to the room. "Get on the bed. I need to take care of you."

"What do you mean?" I aimed my gaze at his shoes.

"Don't ask questions or argue. Just do it."

I stepped toward him, but apparently I wasn't moving fast enough. He took my arm and jerked me to the bed where he bent me over the end.

"Stay still," he snapped.

I squeezed my eyes shut and shivered as his hands slid over my sore bottom. He rubbed in some sort of cream.

"I'm sorry," he said, his voice gruff. "I shouldn't have punished you while I was drunk, but I didn't leave any welts."

This time.

He finished and stepped back, and a set of clothing landed by my head on the mattress. "Get dressed."

"We need to talk," I said, my voice cracking as I reached for the clothes. I was too close to splitting in two, and I didn't know if I could handle talking to him right now, but I had to try. I had to do something to relieve this ache in my heart, to make him understand he was wrong.

"We have nothing to talk about. You need to get dressed and leave."

My eyes widened as I pulled on a pair of jeans. "What?"

"You can take the car, the credit card—take what you want. I don't care about any of it. Use it as long as you need to, but don't come back here or call." He moved to the other side of the bed, as if he couldn't tolerate our proximity.

"So that's it?" I said, my voice wavering as I slipped into a T-shirt. "You're just going to send me away?"

"You're carrying that bastard's kid!" Seizing the lamp on the nightstand, he hurtled it across the room. The ceramic busted, echoing its haunting death through the basement. "I hate it, and I hate you. Now get the fuck out of my house and take Eve"—his voice cracked on her name—"with you."

Numbness stole over me. I couldn't process. He'd revealed so many sides of himself, so many personalities that all meshed to make up this complex, passionate, cruel, beautiful man in front of me. But this side of him...I hated this side of him as intensely as he now hated me.

"Go!" he screamed. "I can't stand the sight of you!"

I'd never seen him so livid, so destroyed by what he thought I'd done. I could have fallen to pieces at his feet, could have begged him to put me back together again. To make me whole. But I wouldn't. This was my chance to wash him from my life. Truly start over. Eve would be fine without him. I would be fine without him. The baby we'd created together, the one he hated, would be fine without him.

"Okay," I whispered, forcing my shaky limbs to move. I picked up the bag he'd tossed on the floor, pulled my purse strap high onto my shoulder, and headed toward the stairs. I said nothing; he wouldn't listen anyway. The man I knew was gone. I didn't know this stranger who had just cast me aside like I was nothing. Gage Channing had made me feel a lot of things in the time I'd known him, but never this—like I meant nothing to him.

I clutched the bag, knuckles turning to ash as the pain threatened to choke me. My whole body was ash. He'd incinerated me. A month ago, I wouldn't have thought it possible, but I loved him, and his hate almost brought me to my knees. Devastation welled in my throat, and I grabbed hold of my last thread of strength. I would not break down in front of him. I wouldn't.

"Wait," he said.

My lifeless feet halted on the first step. Slowly, I turned, a pang of hope fisting my heart.

His mouth never strayed from the mean line it formed. "My mother's ring." He marched to where I stood and held out his hand. "I want it back."

I blinked several times as I slid the ring down my finger, and I made the mistake of meeting his eyes as I dropped it into his waiting palm. That seething hatred wrecked what was left of me.

"You're the last woman on Earth who deserves to wear her ring." And with a wave of his hand, he dismissed me.

Just like that.

And I didn't know how I kept from breaking on the spot.

18. PURGATORY

We left before sunrise, and my tears fell in an endless stream once Eve and I sped down the road. I had a full tank of gas, a credit card with unlimited capabilities, and nowhere to go. No one to turn to. So I just drove, practically on autopilot because I was aware of nothing.

Only the hum of the road underneath me and the trickle of rain splashing the windshield.

Eventually, the flow of heartbreak slowed, and I realized I'd looped downtown Portland on the freeways twice when the first hint of pain began in my lower back. I straightened in the driver's seat and tried to get comfortable, but my head swam.

God, pull it together, Kayla.

Eve slept in the backseat. I glanced into the rearview, noticing how uncomfortable she looked with her head hanging over the edge of the car seat. I couldn't be a wreck when she awoke. Wiping my eyes, I looped the city again and gave myself time to calm down, but it didn't help much, especially when the traffic on the 405 came to a standstill.

Wonderful.

My stomach grumbled, and I was sure Eve must have been hungry too since we'd left *his* house without eating. Traffic inched forward at an agonizing pace—morning rush hour traffic at its finest for sure. My stomach grumbled again, this time accompanied by cramping that gripped my right side with the strength of pliers. I squeezed the steering wheel and told myself everything was okay.

It'd been a couple of stressful days, and I remembered cramping during my pregnancy with Eve. My stomach was too empty; I'd thrown up again before leaving his driveway and had gotten a bit of satisfaction at leaving my nasty bile on his pavement.

Pain spread through my abdomen, and my pulse sped up, thundering in my ears as I drew air into my lungs. This was more than hunger pains. The black interior of the car wavered, as if I saw it through warped glass, and a dull ache started in my shoulder. Suddenly weak, I let my head fall back against the headrest and closed my eyes.

Someone honked. Behind me?

I didn't know. Was traffic moving? I couldn't concentrate beyond the pain. Something was wrong, and I thought back to my first pregnancy; the one Rick caused me to miscarry.

Not again.

Last night, Gage had slammed me into the bathroom wall before he'd stalked out, and when he'd returned...

But he hadn't hurt me. Not really. He may have

marked my ass and thighs, but the real damage had been psychological. Someone honked again just as my vision started to fade. Blindly, I reached for my purse, tried to get my hands on my cell as my foot let up on the brake. The car lurched forward and hit something…

I was on my back when I gasped to awareness. My arms and legs thrashed, and someone held them down. Panic cut off my air, and I couldn't make a sound, so where was that screaming coming from? That gut-wrenching crying? Sounded much too young to be me.

Eve.

Eve was crying. Where was she? I needed her by me, needed her hand in mine so she wouldn't be alone and scared. I found my voice but no more than a whimper escaped as my right side lit on fire.

"…into shock! Let's move it!"

Voices, commotion, bodies crowding me, hands reaching, yet I could grab onto nothing. I sucked in each breath, as if through a straw, and a drop of sweat trickled down my face. My whole body heated—too hot, too drenched. I was burning alive where my baby nestled; my tiny baby who had yet to form arms and legs, fingers and toes. Who barely had a heartbeat.

I was losing him, and Eve had asked for a brother last Christmas.

My stomach dropped at the sensation of being lifted, and when I opened my eyes for a second, squinting against the colorful lights that strobed atop the ambulance, I saw the ominous clouds overhead. Thick and grey, they extinguished the brilliance of the rising sun and set the scene perfectly for this day.

"Wh…what's happening?" I managed to say.

"We're taking you to the ER. We're doing everything we can to help you," a deep voice assured.

But the crying hadn't stopped. My poor baby. Why was she crying? "My daughter…"

"She's okay. An officer is taking her to the hospital. Is there someone we can call to meet her?"

"Gage"—I felt myself sinking, much too fast—"Channing." Why had I given his name? He hated me, hated the baby.

The baby…

"I'm pregnant." I moaned as another wave of pain hit. I must be dying, I thought before there was simply… nothing.

19. GONE

A low moan roused me.

"Kayla?"

Someone moaned again, and I realized it was me. I forced my lids open, squinting against the soft light that seared my eyes. "Ian?" I had to be dreaming. Why would he be here? I hadn't heard from him in weeks. In fact, I wasn't even sure where *here* was.

"Hey." His gentle voice came from my left.

I swerved my head and blinked the room into focus. A small and windowless area, partitioned by curtains, enclosed us. Ian sat at my bedside, and I noticed a monitor behind him. "Why..." God, why did talking grate my throat like sandpaper? And why was I in the hospital? At least, I assumed it was a hospital. Sure smelled like one. "Why am I here?"

"How much do you remember?"

"Um..." Driving. Crying. Pain. "I was driving. We were stopped in traffic..." I drew a blank after that, though the feeling I should recall something—a voice assuring me everything would be okay—remained.

And crying. I remembered Eve crying.

"You were on the 405 when you passed out," he said, fingers folding around mine. "Another motorist called 9-1-1."

I squeezed his hand, mainly because I needed to hold onto something, and he just happened to be there. "What happened? Where's Eve?"

His gaze fell. "Did you know you were pregnant?"

Were.

I sucked in a quick breath. "The baby?"

"I'm sorry. Your pregnancy was ectopic." He pulled his hand from mine and wiped both palms down his face, and I realized how exhausted he seemed. "Your tube ruptured. I was the attending when they brought you in. I've never been so scared in my life. They had to rush you into surgery."

I comprehended his words, but mostly I felt numb. "Am I gonna be okay?"

He slumped into the chair. "The internal bleeding wasn't as bad as they feared. You lost some blood, and they couldn't save the tube, but you should recover fine."

"Where's Eve?"

He clenched his jaw. "She's in the waiting room with Gage."

He came.

A nurse appeared from behind the curtain. "Good, you're awake," she said. "They're about to move you to a more comfortable room. Are you in any pain?"

"Um, I don't think so," I said, though I hadn't tried to

move yet either.

She fastened a blood pressure cuff around my arm, and a machine buzzed. "You'll probably feel woozy from the pain meds." She took more vitals and then made notes in a chart. "I'll leave you in Dr. Kaplan's hands." With a smile, she disappeared through the gap in the curtains.

Ian fell eerily silent, and I was too drowsy to ask what was on his mind. I must have dozed off, because they startled me awake when they moved me into a private room. Ian never left my side.

"Aren't you supposed to be working?" I mumbled, rubbing sleep from my eyes.

"My shift was almost over when the ambulance brought you in. You're stuck with me." He settled into a chair and leaned forward. "Kayla," he began hesitantly, resting both elbows on his knees, "we need to talk about the bruises."

"What?"

"On your backside. You're black and"—he cut off and swallowed—"You're black and blue, and I'm pretty sure I know why."

I closed my eyes. "I don't want to talk about it."

"I'm not the only one concerned. The staff here mentioned abuse."

"And you helped them with their assumptions, didn't you?"

"I can't keep quiet about this anymore. He's hurting you. What are you gonna do when he starts in on Eve?"

I jerked into a sitting position, grimacing as pain

seared my abdomen. "Gage would never hurt her."

"He's got you brainwashed—"

"You need to stop *right* now." The warning in my voice must have registered because he gaped at me. "I'm not blind to his ways, and I'm not a pushover either. What's important is how he's treated my daughter, and he's been nothing but good to her."

"And what about you? How does he treat you?"

The echo of Gage's mistrust pained my heart, and I pushed the memory into a hidden compartment of my mind. "What we do in the privacy of our bedroom is none of your business."

"You're in denial."

"No," I choked. "I just lost my baby and the last thing I need is another lecture from you."

"I know you're hurting, but I can't ignore this. Seeing you hurt like that…" He shook his head. "A social worker is waiting to speak with you. You need to talk to her."

"What good is talking to some stranger about my sex life going to do?" I didn't care if my words got under his skin; his burrowed into mine like a chigger.

He winced. "Talk to her. That's all I'm asking."

"I can't believe you got a social worker involved."

"Don't blame me. I didn't leave those bruises on your body."

Regardless of how much Gage had hurt me, he'd stopped when I said the safe word. That had to mean something, right? Or was I so far gone from logic and reason that I didn't recognize good from bad anymore? "I told you I was wrong for you, but you wouldn't listen."

"I did listen!" He sprang to his feet. "I've done my best to move on," he continued, lowering his voice, "but when you're brought into my ER, nearly dead and covered in bruises...I can't handle that. I'm not sorry for loving you, and I won't apologize for saying what you don't want to hear. You need help."

"You need to stay out of this."

His body tensed. "You're a smart, courageous woman, and you've always put Eve first. If I know nothing else about the person you've become, I know that's still true. You can't go back to him. If not for yourself, do it for her."

The sting of fresh tears threatened, but I refused to let them spill. "He doesn't want me anymore."

"What?" He sounded incredulous.

I let out a bitter laugh. "He thinks the baby is...was... yours. He says he can't have kids." I glanced up at him. "Did you know Liz was pregnant?"

The question hit him like a punch to the gut. He stumbled back. "No, she wasn't."

"Gage says she was. He also says the baby was yours."

"That's...nuts. Why wouldn't he tell me?"

"I don't know." I absently played with the edge of the blanket wrapped around my body. "Did he ask to see me?"

"I suspect you know as well as I do that Gage doesn't ask—he demands."

"I want to see him."

"I can't change your mind, can I?"

"We already went over this in Texas. I made my

choice." Well, it'd been made for me, but I wouldn't tell him that. "I care about you, but you need to let me go." I narrowed my eyes. "And you never should have gotten a social worker involved."

"I didn't. Gage's abuse did."

I gritted my teeth. "It's unnecessary. If anyone asks, tell them the truth. I like kinky sex."

"Jesus, Kayla…"

"Can you please send him in? I need to see Eve."

"Fine," he said in a clipped tone. "I'll send the bastard in." He stormed from the room, and not two minutes later, Gage stood in the doorway.

I looked behind him, hoping to spot my daughter's short auburn curls, but she was nowhere in sight. "Where's Eve?"

"Ian took her to the cafeteria," he said as he closed the door. He stepped to my bedside and sank into a chair. "She'll be back in a while. I wanted to speak with you alone first."

"Why? You hate me, remember?"

I jumped when his hand settled over mine. "You need me."

"I needed you yesterday."

He dropped his head onto the thin mattress, next to my hip, and kissed the palm he held. "I don't hate you."

"But you don't trust me."

"We're not doing this now. You just got out of surgery."

"Why not? Ian didn't hold back."

"What are you talking about?"

I snorted. "Apparently, the hospital staff thinks you're abusing me. He wants me to talk to a social worker."

"Maybe you should. Maybe you should tell them everything. You could easily send me back to jail."

"I was willing, Gage."

"That's not entirely true. I kidnapped you, and last night…"

My breath hitched, then shuddered out. "What you did and said hurt, but I knew what I was getting into when I stayed. You gave me the option of leaving, but I stayed." I caught his gaze. "I was willing. You made me admit it, remember?"

"Yes," he murmured. "I remember. I molded you into what I wanted, and then I threw you out at the first sign of trouble."

"Why'd you do it?"

He fell quiet for a few long moments. "It was deja vu, Kayla. I should have punished you for lying to me, but demanding marriage and then making you leave was wrong." He held his mother's ring between two fingers. "This belongs on your finger. No matter what, you are and always will be *mine*." My mouth gaped as he slid the diamond onto my finger—as if he'd never demanded it back to begin with. "I was scared of hurting you," he said. "*Really* hurting you." He paused, avoiding my eyes. "Did I cause your miscarriage? I don't care that it was his, if I made you lose your baby—"

"The baby *wasn't* his!" I yanked my hand from his grasp. "You refuse to believe me, but it's the truth." Sorrow welled in my throat. "The baby was *ours*." Turning away, I buried my face in the pillow and muffled my sobs. I formed a ball, bringing about pain from the incision but instead of recoiling from it, I held on to it, breathed through it until I could think of nothing else.

His voice called to me through my despair, and I tensed when his arms came around me. Gage wasn't the comforting kind.

"I didn't mean to do this…" he cut off, strangled.

"You didn't. It was a tubal pregnancy. A miscarriage was inevitable." His embrace comforted me more than I wanted to admit, especially after what he'd said and done, but I needed his arms to live through the next second, the next minute, the next hour. "Why can't you trust me? You swore nothing happened with Katherine, and I took your word for it. Why can't you do the same?"

"It's not that simple." He withdrew his arms, sat up, and scooted to the edge of the bed, as if he needed distance.

"Then make it simple. God, you made me love you!"

"What else do you want me to say, Kayla?"

"Everything! I want answers. I want to understand why you're so adamant the baby wasn't yours."

He hung his head. "They told me back in high school I can't have kids. I sustained a lot of damage from…it doesn't matter."

"Damage from what?"

"A nasty brawl with the bastard my mother married."

A beat of heavy silence weighed on us, and I hurt for him as much as I did for myself in that moment. "Why didn't you tell me?"

"Because telling you would have led to this! You and your questions. I try not to think about the past, and I sure as hell don't talk about it."

"But you put me on birth control…" I shook my head as nothing about this made sense. "Why would you do that if you thought you couldn't father children?"

"I gave you a placebo, Kayla. I *can't* father children."

"Obviously, you can," I snapped. "Whoever diagnosed you made a mistake, or something changed—"

"I'm not discussing this with you," he interrupted. "You need to focus on recovering."

"I didn't sleep with him! It's only been you—in four fucking years, Gage, it's been you!"

The door opened, and Ian appeared in the entrance with Eve. Gage stood, his gaze dark and dangerous. He was still full of rage—toward me, toward his brother. "They tell me you're being released tomorrow," he said. "Call me. I'll come get you." He stepped around Ian, glaring at him the whole time, and closed the door upon his exit.

"You okay?" Ian asked.

"Yeah," I lied. I held my breath as Eve dawdled to my bedside, her head down, and told myself to get a grip. I wasn't about to fall apart in front of my daughter. "I'm sorry I scared you, baby." I scooted over and patted the space next to me, and she hopped up. "Mommy's okay." I tilted her chin up. "Okay?"

She nodded. "Are we going home with Gage?"

I blinked, my lids becoming heavy from the pain meds they'd given me. Instead of answering her, I glanced at Ian. "Thanks for watching her."

"No problem."

Eve cuddled into my side, and almost instantly, she fell asleep. "She must have been so scared," I said.

"She's a trooper like her mom." He wandered around the small room, and silence fell on us for a while. "I don't understand why you put yourself through this."

"It's...complicated."

"Don't give me that," he said quietly, though the vehemence in his tone hinted at frustration.

"You won't like the truth."

He let out a bitter laugh. "I'm sure I won't, but I think I deserve it."

"I love him."

"You loved Rick at one time too."

"It's different. Gage and I have our issues, but he's not Rick."

"No, he is exactly like Rick. Abuse is abuse. You're smart enough to know this, but you're letting sex get in the way of your thinking."

"I'm not talking about this with you. It's not fair to you, and I just don't have the energy." I brushed my hair from my eyes, and his gaze lingered on my hand.

Shit. I'd forgotten about the ring.

He strode to my side, snatched my hand between his, and glared at the diamond, as if he could make it disappear. "I should have been the one to put this on your finger. I can't believe you're actually going to marry him. Are you insane?"

"Please, don't do this."

"He has no remorse, Kayla, and he knows nothing about loving someone."

I pulled my hand from his. "That's not true. I've seen sides of him I would have sworn didn't exist a year ago. I can't help the way I feel, Ian."

"Me neither, so where does that leave us?"

"Nowhere."

He nodded, his mouth forming a tight line. "Okay. I get it." He opened the door, and his face and movements spoke of resignation as he exited the room. I'd gotten my wish—he'd given up. I'd just destroyed my first love, a decade long friendship, and I couldn't even muster a tear. I didn't have any left.

20. FINDING HOME

Two weeks.

That was how long Gage shut me out after he brought me home. That word bothered me. This was no longer home, and Gage was no longer the man who lit my world on fire. I didn't know who this stranger was— this cold and detached man who couldn't bring himself to touch me.

At least where Eve was concerned, he hadn't changed. Clearly, he'd won her over again in the hospital, because she'd resumed shadowing him. They got closer every day, while he and I grew further apart.

He was in the wrong, and I should be furious at the things he'd said and done, at his refusal to believe the baby was his, but I experienced nothing but despair. I preferred him yelling or screaming; wished he'd bend me over his knee and beat me if it meant he'd feel *something*. As the days wore on and I slowly recovered, his indifference squeezed the last bit of warmth from my soul. I might as well have been back in that basement, my heart bleeding as his hatred lanced me.

The nights were the worst—the darkest hours being the darkest in my mind. He slept beside me, but we never touched. Never kissed. Never talked. I lay next to him for hours, inches from his heat but unable to take comfort in it, and I tortured myself with memories of the night he'd beat me with the bullwhip...and the fact that I'd lost another baby.

Being shut out like this...it sucked the life from me, and I'd done nothing to deserve it.

I couldn't take it anymore. The first time I waited on my knees for him, I'd hoped for even a marginal reaction; a stiffening of his muscles, a clenched jaw—anything—but he barely gave me a second glance as he ordered me into bed. Ignoring his command, I waited on the hardwood long after he shut off the light and slid between the sheets, and eventually I crawled in beside him, holding my breath to stanch the flow of sorrow. My tears drenched my pillow that night.

The following evening I did the same—waited on my knees and prepared to go to battle. I'd rather him furious than indifferent. He made me wait a long time, which I guessed was his way of avoiding my display of submission.

"What are you doing?" he demanded as he came into our bedroom and closed the door. "I thought I made myself clear last night." Like he did every night, he shed his clothes and headed for the bathroom. The door slammed shut behind him. I glanced at my ring, wondering why it still decorated my finger, wondering why I was still here if he no longer wanted me.

He opened the door a few minutes later, and I still hadn't moved. "Get up, Kayla." He strode to where I knelt, his cock standing proud, though apparently he had no intention of using it. I fisted his shaft, earning a low growl from him.

"Please," I said, raising my eyes to his, "Master." I paused, waiting for a reaction to that word. He gave none. "Let me suck you off." I closed my mouth around him, and he immediately shoved me back. I lost my balance and fell on my butt.

"Get up," he said through clenched teeth. Our breaths came fast and heavy, and I thought he was about to say something more, but he stepped away and headed for the bed, leaving me on my ass in the middle of the room. I wiped my eyes and got to my feet.

"Maybe I *should* fuck him, since you believe I did. I might as well do the deed and deserve the bastard way you've been treating me."

He whirled, grabbed me, and slammed me to the mattress. "You don't see him, you don't talk to him"—his fingers clamped around my wrists, and he wrenched them above my head—"you don't fucking *think* about him."

"I don't, Gage. I don't think about him at all. All I can think about is you and the way you've shut me out. It's killing me. Please. I'll call you Master again, I'll let you beat me with the bullwhip. I'll do whatever you want, just stop hurting me like this."

He blinked several times. "I...can't."

"Why can't you trust me?"

Loosening his grip, he turned his back and mumbled, "Go to sleep."

Tears silently streamed down my face, and I held my breath to keep quiet as we settled under the covers. I didn't know what to do, didn't know how to get beyond the wall he'd constructed. How could we work through this if he wouldn't talk to me?

Desperation took over, and I spread my thighs, slid my fingers between them, and rubbed my clit. I almost came on the spot—that's how sexually frustrated he'd left me. A cry escaped, but I focused on drawing out the pleasure. He'd taught me a lot about control. I opened wider and hooked a foot over his calf, and I blatantly worked myself toward orgasm.

Blatantly disobeyed him.

He kicked my foot off and turned to face me. His eyes darkened, narrowed.

I didn't stop. Let him be pissed. Let him punish me for masturbating. I didn't care. My eyes fluttered shut, and I moaned again.

"Look at me while you disobey me. I want to see your shame when you come."

Cheeks flooding with embarrassment, I arched my spine as my climax pulsed around my fingers. The blanket fell below my breasts, and my nipples puckered in the chilly room, begging for his hot mouth. I crashed from the high, my gaze connected to his, and the awkwardness of the moment wasn't lost on me. I withdrew my hand, but he pushed my fingers back into silky, wet heat.

"Come for me again, until it's painful, until you think

you can't stand it anymore. Work your wet cunt, Kayla. Dip your fingers in and see what you've done to yourself."

"I…I don't think I can…"

"Oh yes, you can."

"Please, Gage…"

"Do it now."

I worked myself toward another orgasm and held my breath as the pressure built. My whole body shuddered and pulsed, and his groan only added to the intensity. Finally, a reaction.

"Again," he said, his voice hoarse.

He made me rub myself into multiple orgasms, and I didn't think I had it in me to come again until he sucked a nipple into his mouth. He covered my fingers with his, pressing hard on my clit, and literally forced my hand. An overpowering wave of pain seized my body.

"Stop, it hurts!" I cried.

"Keep going."

He pressed harder, keeping my hand in place. I writhed, squirmed…pleaded as moisture trickled down my cheeks. "I…I…please…can't."

"You can and you will."

I vocalized the pain in strangled grunts, openly sobbing as I came again. "Stop hating me."

"I don't hate you." He scooted away so we didn't touch at all. "Now stop pushing me and go to sleep."

"I didn't sleep with him," I choked. "It was your baby. Stop hating me for losing it."

"God, Kayla," he said, abruptly crushing me in his

arms. "I don't hate you—I fucking hate myself!" He buried his face in my shoulder, and his body trembled as he held me. We stayed like that for a long time, his body wrapped around mine, shuddering with the emotion he'd bottled up since I'd come home from the hospital.

"I can't face what I said to you. I told you I hated it, told you I hated you."

"Gage…"

"I'm so fucked up." Something wet trickled down the side of my neck, and I was stunned to realize it was his tears. "I know it was mine. I didn't want to admit it, didn't want to face the monster I'd become. I'm sorry, baby. I don't deserve you."

"Deserve me then," I whispered. "Love me again. I'm dying without you."

His lips found mine, and he rolled me to my back, wedged my legs apart, and slipped inside where he belonged.

And it was like coming home.

He trapped my hands above my head and nipped at my neck, brushed his lips across my breasts, opened his mouth over first one nipple then the other, and like always, his body owned me. His thighs nestled between mine, rubbing my skin as he pushed into me with patience, though I knew he needed to come. It had been long for him too, these past two weeks.

"Fuck, Kayla," he said, voice ragged as he spilled into me with a violent thrust. His deep groan filled the air, and afterward, for the first time in what seemed like forever, he cocooned me in his embrace.

Definitely like coming home.

We lay in quiet harmony for a while, though neither of us slept. I played with the diamond on my finger, sliding it to the knuckle then down again. "You put your ring back on my finger, so I'm assuming you still expect me to marry you?"

"Damn right, I do. I made a mistake, and now it's rectified."

"This is what you call fixing things? Keeping your distance for two weeks, refusing to talk to me, and then pretending nothing's wrong?"

"I didn't trust myself with you."

"How will you ever trust me if you can't trust yourself?"

"Good question." He sighed. "Tell me what to do, Kayla, and I'll do it. I don't want to hurt you anymore."

"Go to counseling."

"So you think a shrink is the answer?"

I practically heard the scowl in his tone. "I don't know what the answer is, but I can't do this anymore. I can handle…tolerate…your rules and your need to hurt me physically, but I can't handle you not trusting me. I can't handle you shutting me out—not when I've given you everything." I grasped his arms and forced my next words out. "Either get help, or let me go for good."

Please, don't let me go.

"Okay."

"Okay?" I raised a brow.

"I'll get…help." He tightened his hold on me. "As soon as you marry me."

"I'll marry you as soon as you trust me."

"I do trust you."

"No, you don't."

"I'm working on it."

"Then prove it."

"And how do you suggest I do that?"

He had a point. Trust was something not only earned but shown through action, and he had a long way to go. What was the one thing he trusted no one with? My heart skipped a beat.

Control.

That was his Achilles heel—the single thing he never gave up because it left him too vulnerable. If he had to choose between his millions and control, I suspected he'd choose the latter.

"Submit to me for one night."

He laughed. "That will never happen, Kayla. I submit to no one."

"Then I can't marry you."

"Of course you can."

"Do you love me, Gage?"

"That's a stupid question."

I shook my head. "No, it's not. Ian wanted one night, and I tried, but in the end I didn't love him enough. Do you love me enough? You're asking for everything. You expect me to hand over my entire life to you—my free will, my decisions, my body. Give me yours for one night," I said, my voice going soft. "All I'm asking for is one night. Prove you can give me your trust, and I'll marry you."

"One night?"

I nodded.

"And what do you plan to do on this *one* night?"

My pulse sped up as all kinds of wicked things went through my head, though there was only one thing I really wanted from him, and if I could pull this off, he'd give it to me. He'd hate me for it, probably make my ass black and blue afterward, but it would be worth it.

"Guess you'll have to wait and see."

21. MISTRESS

This felt wrong, but God if I wasn't tingling at the thought of making him submit. The idea was exhilarating, arousing…absolutely terrifying. We stood in the middle of the basement, three feet apart from each other, yet the aura of his presence wrapped around me as tangibly as his arms. I was a moment away from sinking to my knees and saying I'd changed my mind.

His lips quirked. "You can't do it, can you?"

I balled my hands. "Strip."

His smile never wavered from amused as he unbuttoned his shirt. "You're nervous. I can read you well. Having second thoughts?"

"I always have second thoughts when it comes to you, so obviously you don't read me well enough."

He let his shirt fall to the floor and then reached for his belt. "What are you going to do with me, now that you have me here under your control?"

We both knew it was a lie. I didn't have control. Not yet. "Give me your belt."

He pulled it from his pant loops and tossed it to me. My mouth parted, breath moistening my lips as he lowered his slacks. Did anything fail to turn him on? His cock stood tall and proud. Suddenly, I lost my inhibitions.

Payback was a bitch.

"Lie on the bed."

"There are many ways to lie on a bed, Kayla."

Didn't I know it. "On your back."

He did so without a word, without shame, and his gaze followed me across the room. I found his leather cuffs and returned to him. I wasn't nearly as capable as he in restraining someone, but I managed to bind his hands to the headboard. I stood back and eyed him.

"Is this all you got?" he asked.

Dropping the belt, I laughed to cover my nervousness and retreated another step, far enough so he could see me from head to toe. I unzipped my dress and let it pool around my feet, revealing nothing underneath except for a pair of thigh highs and a garter belt. No panties. I still obeyed that rule, mainly because it would drive him wild.

His gaze lowered to the lace tops of my stockings, and his appreciation heated my skin. "God, you're sexy."

Fingers trembling, I lightly pinched my nipples, watching him the whole time. Truth was, I had no idea what to do, and I was scared of going to him. He still owned me, even though he was the one cuffed to the damn headboard this time.

Stop being a coward.

I sauntered to the bed and climbed up, my thighs sliding along his as I straddled him. "I'm going to tease you until you beg." I brought my hands to my breasts again, thumbs brushing the peaks until they pebbled into aching buds. His lips parted, as if he were about to speak, but he mashed them together instead. I stared at him, amazed at the sight of him restrained and helpless underneath me.

I dipped my fingers between folds already slick with need and stroked myself while he watched. His chest rose and fell more rapidly as my breathing escalated, and when I came, throwing my head back and arching my spine, I heard him groan.

"You want to come, don't you?" I said, moving down his body and lowering my head, my lips an inch from his wet tip. I raised my eyes to his.

"What do you think, Kayla?"

"I think you're about to beg." I darted my tongue out and lapped up his moisture.

He sucked in a breath. "You know what your mouth does to me."

"You're not coming tonight."

He flexed his hands in the restraints, his eyes deepening to indigo, and my heart pounded. I was going to pay for this, had known it all along, but that hadn't stopped me from strong-arming him into those leather cuffs. The fact that he was playing along with my pathetic attempt at making him submit said a lot.

But he'd still make me pay, especially after what I was about to do. I didn't have the sadist gene, and he had it in spades. I would hurt him though—I'd force his secrets from him and deal with the consequences later.

"You're not coming," I repeated, "unless you give me what I want."

"What do you want?"

"Everything." I licked down his shaft, tongue caressing silky skin, and kissed my way back to the tip. He groaned, his cock twitching under my tongue.

"I'm going to make your ass so red for this," he said through clenched teeth. He looked ready to either devour me, or make me hurt. He'd probably do both simultaneously if I freed him.

"I'm sure you will, but I want answers, Gage, so it's worth it to me."

"What are you talking about?"

Instead of answering, I took him deep, and he raised his hips, his hands bunching into fists as I worked him the way he liked. His body language spoke to me. He was close, his desire trickling out with each slide of my mouth. I curled my fingers around the base of his shaft and squeezed, grazing my teeth just under the head.

A warning.

He closed his eyes, his muscles strung tight as a guitar string. I held still, refusing to give him release, my teeth hinting at pain if he moved an inch. His eyes popped open when I got to my knees. I had all kinds of questions I wanted to ask—things he'd never tell me normally. I had him by the balls, literally, and I wasn't going to waste this opportunity.

"How long did you plan this, before I stole from you?"

"Fuck, Kayla. You're really going there?"

"I'm going there." I fisted his erection and worked him with my hand. "Answer me. How long?"

His hips rose and fell. "Years. Long before I hired you. He wanted you, so I did too."

"You hiring me…that wasn't a coincidence, was it?"

"No."

"Why'd you wait so long to make your move?"

"No opportunity," he gasped. "Put your mouth on me again."

"No. You're not the one in control this time."

"Shit," he said, strangled, "when it comes to you, I'm never in control. Haven't you figured that out yet?"

I paused. "That makes two of us."

"Don't stop, baby. I need your mouth."

I withdrew my hand, ignoring his protests, and circled my clit, though finding release a second time would take longer. "Doing what you did to me…did it help? Do you hate them less now?"

"Them?"

"Ian and his father."

"I can't believe you just said his name while you're straddling me, flicking your damn clit."

I imagined Gage's hands and mouth on my breasts and moaned.

"If you're thinking of him—"

"I'm thinking of you," I interrupted, glancing at his stiff cock. Not even our conversation turned him off. "Answer my question. Do you hate them less?"

"No."

"So it was for nothing, then?"

"I got you, didn't I?"

I sighed as the pressure at my core built. "You got me, so let it go. Hating him does nothing." I squeezed my eyes shut and focused because my next question wasn't going to be easy for either of us. "How bad did his father hurt you?"

"We're not going there. *Ever.*"

"Yes, we are. I want your trust, Gage. Trust me enough to talk about it."

"Not while your cunt is leaking all over my thighs."

I laughed. "After the messed up shit you've put me through, I think you can handle it."

He exhaled. "He beat me. Belts, paddles, sticks—anything he could get his hands on. But my mom...for years I was too young to stop it. So you see, I know exactly how much it hurts."

"Why do you do it, then?"

"Before Liz, I didn't. I hurt myself instead."

His confession broke my composure. My hand fell away, and my eyes burned as I looked down at him.

"Don't feel sorry for me," he snapped. "I've never touched a woman who didn't want it—until you. I knew exactly what I was doing when I forced you into that contract. I'm beyond salvation, so don't think you can fix me."

"You don't need to be fixed. You just need to be loved."

"Kayla, I need to be fucked. Stop toying with me."

"You don't give the orders tonight." I reclaimed the wet, throbbing place between my legs. Later, I'd torture myself with what he'd revealed, but for now I concentrated on the touch of my hand, the heat of his thighs, and remembered the exquisite sensation of his mouth on me. My hoarse cries worked him into a crazed beast. He yanked on the cuffs and drew his knees up before I could stop him. His powerful thighs wrapped around me, and he locked his ankles, holding me prisoner while I worked myself toward another orgasm. His cock nestled against his abdomen, solid and dripping his need all over his skin in wax-like art.

My climax washed over me, a shuddering wave of intensity that gave him the upper hand. He tightened his legs and lifted, and I'd barely caught my breath when he pushed into me. I kicked from his grasp and crawled up his chest. "You're horrible at obeying. I didn't say you could fuck me."

"Free my hands," he said with a growl. "I need to touch you."

I smiled. "Don't like submitting? You make me do it all the time."

He smirked. "Enjoy this while you can. I assure you —you'll never get me here again."

I didn't doubt it for a second. I lowered my lips to his, and he forced them apart and sucked my tongue into his mouth. He might be helpless beneath me, but he made me submit in that kiss.

"You want me to beg?" he said, breathless as he wrenched his mouth from mine. "Fine. I'll beg. Please, let me go so I can punish your fine little ass and fuck you until you scream."

"Hmm, that does sound tempting," I said, "especially when you talk dirty." I brought my lips to his ear. "But I'm not about to waste this night. Now shush—you're balls aren't blue enough yet."

22. INFINITY

I kept him awake most of the night, his hands fisted and body rigid in a constant state of arousal. Considering what he'd done to me a few weeks ago, I couldn't say I felt bad about it. But the instant I released him, he pinned me to the mattress, and a slew of filth left his mouth as he fucked me like a hungry, uncaged tiger. He was saving the red ass for later, he'd promised.

Now we sat at the breakfast table with Eve, and I didn't miss the curve of his mouth every time he looked at me. Obviously, he had diabolical ideas running through his head, though if his preoccupation with punishing me kept him from pressing for a wedding date, I'd let him have his fun.

He'd done what I asked. He'd given me his body for one night, but I still wasn't ready to marry him. A large part of me was getting there, but he failed to understand the small part that still bled from his actions and words. I couldn't just turn those feelings off, no matter how far he went to prove himself.

I waved to Eve as the bus pulled away, and for the longest time I stood in the driveway, oblivious to the rain.

"Come inside," Gage said. "You're going to get sick."

"That's a myth, you know. Rain doesn't make you sick. Viruses and bacteria do."

"Okay smart ass, inside now. We have three hours before she returns, and I'm not going to waste them. Go to the basement and prepare for me."

"Gage, I—"

"Don't argue with me," he interrupted. "I've gone soft on you, but no more. You need to be reminded of who's submitting here, Kayla."

I gazed up at him, taking in the water dripping from his hair and into the collar of his jacket. He'd never looked sexier. I stepped passed him and headed toward the house. "Yes, Master."

"What did you say?"

"You heard me." I hurried through the door and left a trail of water and clothing in my wake. I didn't waste time in the bathroom, and when his feet thumped down the staircase, I not only knelt on the floor, but I had my nose to the hardwood. He was going to hurt me—I knew it with certainty—yet I couldn't contain the flutter of excitement in my stomach. It had been so long since he'd truly wielded his authority over me. His dominance and sadism had taken a backseat to my recovery.

But I knew he was hungry for it, and I was ashamed to admit I was too. I wanted him to take me.

He didn't speak as he neared me, though I sensed him removing his shirt. The heat of his body warmed my skin as he pulled my arms behind my back. He'd never tied them this way before—at the elbows and wrists. His fingers curled around my shoulders.

"Get up." He helped me to my feet. "Spread your legs."

I did as told. He knelt down and fastened a spreader bar between my ankles, and then he disappeared from sight. He wrenched my arms straight out behind me, raising them painfully high and attaching the binding to a hook in the ceiling. The position forced me down, bent at the waist. I dropped my head, and my hair nearly brushed the floor.

"How does that feel?" he asked.

"It hurts." Blood rushed to my brain, making me dizzy, so I lifted my head.

"Good. It's supposed to." He pulled out a set of nipple clamps.

"Please, no."

"No safe words during punishment."

"What am I being punished for?"

"I'm punishing you," he said as he clamped one nipple before moving to the other, "for getting yourself off so many times last night while leaving me in agony. For making me talk about things I had no plans of ever discussing with you."

I winced. These clamps were the worst yet; they had weights dangling from them. I sucked in a breath. "You're a hypocrite."

"No, I simply know my place. You do too, or you wouldn't have had your nose to the floor. You knew this was coming."

"What are you going to do to me?"

"Whatever I please."

I closed my eyes long enough to catch my breath, which was a mistake because I never saw the gag coming. This one was different; it forced my mouth open in a perfect "O" big enough for his cock to fit through. He stepped back, and I peeked up through my hair, my legs shaking under the pressure of keeping balance.

"I do love the sight of you like this. You're so vulnerable right now."

Reaching for his belt, he unbuckled it and lowered the zipper of his pants. He fisted my hair, urging my head up, and slipped his cock through the opening in the gag.

"You have the sweetest mouth," he said, breathless. His hips rocked slowly at first before he jackhammered in and out of my mouth.

The taste of him turned me on, and if not for the gag, I would have closed my lips around him and worked him hard. Would have made *his* knees tremble the way mine did. His release hit me in a gush, but I had trouble swallowing with my jaw locked wide open. He let go of my hair, and I dropped my head, watching as his cum dribbled from my mouth onto the floor. He wiped my chin with a washcloth, and then he stepped back and pulled the belt from his pants.

I suddenly feared that belt. I couldn't say why, as I'd grown used to it during the few weeks we'd had together before I'd found out I was pregnant, but now, the thought of him using it made me cry. I squeezed my eyes shut, and my tears were lost in my hair. The first strike was soft, a warm up. As the second one landed, harder, on the back of my thighs, I realized why this lashing reduced me to a blubbering mess.

All I could think about was the baby I'd lost, and how he'd said he hated it. I trembled from the force of my sobs as drool dripped down my chin. The sounds coming from me were gut wrenching and deep, and I couldn't hide them.

He removed the clamps and gag, pushed the hair from my eyes, and cradled my face, his thumbs brushing away the tears. "Tell me what's wrong."

"I...I can't...can't do this now. All I can think about is..."

"The baby," he said, regret strangling his tone, "and the way I treated you that night."

Another sob hitched, and as he moved behind me and freed my arms, a wave of guilt overcame me, swift and dark and suffocating. I hadn't cried enough over the loss; I'd locked the grief away instead. Now it choked me. He removed the spreader bar and then carried me to bed. His body spooned mine, both arms wrapping me in his embrace, and I thought about how he'd stopped. He could have ignored my tears and kept going—it's what he would have done in the past.

But this wasn't the Gage I'd known back then.

"Do you think about the baby?"

"All the time," he said, voice rough and deep. "But I try not to. That night...it was one of the darkest moments of my life, and I hate to think I contributed to what you went through."

"You've changed."

"Or maybe you didn't know me before."

I shook my head. "No, something's changed."

"I had too much time to think in prison."

"About?" I laced my fingers with his.

"Eleven months, twenty-five days, four hours, and thirty-nine minutes—that's how long it took to realize what you mean to me. You make me want to be a better person, Kayla. No one's done that in a very long time."

"Did you consider that while you were kidnapping me?"

"I wasn't considering much of anything. I couldn't get the image of you and *him* out of my fucking head. So yes, I went crazy. Haven't you figured out by now that crazy is what I do best?"

I let out a breath. "You could say that."

"I won't apologize for who I am, for loving you this way."

I found his words eerily similar to Ian's in the hospital. "I don't expect an apology from you, Gage. I know better."

"But I *am* sorry."

I stiffened. "But you just said…"

"I know what I said, and I meant it. But I'm sorry I said those things to you, sorry I took back the ring. It belongs on your finger, and you belong to me, so let's set a date already."

"I'm not ready."

"Kayla…" He paused, taking a deep breath. "Pick a

date, or I'll pick one for us, but this isn't negotiable. We're getting married."

"You're not being fair!" I pushed against his arms, but he only held on tighter.

"I'm rarely fair, but I am your Master and you will obey me. Now pick a damn date—any date in the next few weeks."

"You pick it, since you're in such a hurry."

"Baby, I submitted to you last night. That was the deal. Now pick a date, or I *will* take my belt to your ass, and I won't stop this time, no matter how much you cry."

"Why do have to be such a bastard?"

"It's in my nature." He fell silent for a beat. "Do you still love me?"

"Define *love*."

He rolled us over and pinned me, but his deep blue eyes did the job just as effectively. "It's all-consuming, leaves me unable to breath when I look at you, and when you submit, truly submit your very being to me, there's no better feeling in the world. That's when I know you love me—when you lie in wait of my every whim and desire. I don't give a fuck what the world thinks of us, Kayla, but we need each other. Tell me when you'll marry me."

"As soon as you want," I whispered.

His lips claimed mine, and we became a tangle of tongues and limbs as our bodies came together.

"You overwhelm me," I gasped. "Gage…I'm gonna come."

"Not yet," he moaned. "Not until I give you permission." He held my wrists in one hand above my head as he sank into me, again and again with slow madness.

"Oh God…you're killing me."

"That's the idea." His mouth curved into his devil's grin before he sucked a nipple between his teeth.

"What will you do…if I come anyway?" I was about to, if he didn't stop teasing my breasts with his mouth and fingers.

"I'll deny you for a week."

"I hate you."

"You love me."

"I do," I said, arching as my toes curled.

"Then come for me."

Thank God he gave me permission because I was a goner anyway.

A long while later, he still lingered inside me, and his lips and hands never stopped exploring my body. He left a wet path down my neck.

"Eve will be back soon," I said with a sigh.

"I know." He placed one last kiss on my lips before sliding from bed. We showered and dressed in under ten minutes, and I was just about to climb the stairs when he stopped me.

"Wait. I have something for you." He opened a drawer, pulled out a box, and came toward me. Removing a necklace from the black velvet encasing, he said, "It's an infinity collar." The choker appeared to be made of stainless steel and minimalist in design, save for the diamonds sparkling in the symbol at the front.

"Do you like it?"

"It's beautiful."

He inserted a key into the discreet lock on the backside and opened the collar. "Get on your knees."

I dropped to my knees and clasped my hands at the small of my back.

He swept my hair aside and fastened the choker around my throat. "You make the collar beautiful, Kayla. You'll always be mine, and this piece of jewelry, to which only I hold the key, signifies that. We'll exchange rings during the ceremony, but this is the true token of our relationship. Our love never ends, and neither does my possession of you." He tilted my chin up. "So if you want to back out, do it now."

"Leaving would be the sane thing to do, but you're under my skin, Gage Channing. You've shown me there's a good man hiding somewhere inside your rotten soul."

He grinned. "Don't tell anyone."

23. OVER THE ROSE PETALS

"Are you sure about this?"

"I'm sure," I said as Stacey adjusted my veil. She'd flown in yesterday, and besides Gage and Eve, she was the only person I knew at my own wedding. The rest of the guests, acquaintances and business associates of Gage's, were only there to bear witness to the wedding of the year.

That's what the local media called it, anyway.

"Okay, then," she said. "Let's get this show on the road." She knelt and straightened the hem of Eve's dress that matched my own. "You know what to do, right, hon?

My daughter nodded, a wide grin on her face.

The music filtered into the back where Stacey had fawned over me as I'd gotten ready. She left the room and walked down the aisle, followed by Eve. I waited, wringing my fingers and shuffling my feet. The first strains of Pachelbel's "Canon in D" began, and I stepped outside the sanctuary of my hiding place.

Everyone stood and faced me, their eyes widening as

I came into view. Amongst a chorus of "oohhs and aahhs," I scanned the audience and gave a sigh of relief that Ian was nowhere to be found. Deep down, I feared he'd make an appearance and try to stop the wedding, but he really had given up. The realization caused a pang of sadness in me; I hated how things had ended between us. Mostly, I hated the way I'd hurt him.

I walked over the rose petals Eve sprinkled in her wake, bringing me one, two, three steps closer to *him*. I sensed the heat of his gaze and finally lifted my eyes to his. Oh God…I'd forgotten how well Gage Channing wore a tux. A shiver ran through me at his expression; it encompassed so many things—smoldering desire, lethal resolve, but above all else, ownership. I was his, and this ceremony was only a technicality to make sure the world realized it too.

That walk was the longest of my life, but when I joined him and we laced our fingers together, the significance of the moment left me in awe. I was being reborn from the ashes he'd created.

The wedding officiator recited his introduction and then the vows began.

"Gage Channing, do you take Kayla Sutton to be your wife, to love, honor, and cherish now and forever more?"

"I do," he said, his gaze never leaving mine.

He would push me beyond my limits, always demand more than I wanted to give, but damn if he didn't make me feel alive. I needed him to breathe, and my humiliation and submission were small prices to pay. My body would endure him, because without him it would petrify.

"Kayla Sutton, do you take Gage Channing to be your husband, to love, honor, and obey..."

Obey.

Gage's mouth curved into a satisfied smile. The man performing the ceremony had no idea the weight that word carried in our relationship. Above all else, I would obey him.

"...now and forever more?"

My heart thumped—a drumming beat that grew louder with every second obey flitted through my mind. Obey and owned. Two little words, both beginning with the same letter but holding so much meaning in the complexity of our union.

Gage waited for my answer, his sapphire eyes alight with absolute confidence. I was his.

His to command. His to set on fire. His to punish.

His.

I cleared my throat, parted my lips, and confirmed in front of God and the world what Gage and I already knew.

"I do."

His.

Now and forever more.

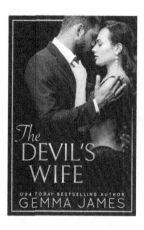

No one claims marriage is easy. That is especially true for Kayla Sutton, because she's married to a sadist who takes the meaning of the word "dominance" to new heights.

But Kayla should have known. She fell for his wicked ways after he blackmailed her, stayed after he kidnapped her, and went back to him after he almost destroyed them both with his fury.

Then she married him.

A year has passed since Kayla agreed to love, honor, and obey. Day after day, she survives his volatile nature—on her knees at his feet, underneath him between the sheets, and bent over the bed to receive the lash of his belt. But she's beginning to miss the one thing she promised Gage Channing when she married him.

Her freedom.

Please visit my website to find where you can purchase The Devil's Wife: www.authorgemmajames.com/books

Acknowledgments

A special thanks to the readers and bloggers who emailed me, stalked me on Facebook, and let me know they wanted more of Kayla's story. This one is for you guys! I owe a lot of gratitude to the following people: Janet Taylor-Perry, who edited the book and caught the errors I was blind to; Franny and Silvia at Dark World Books for their unwavering support and encouragement; Debra at Book Enthusiast Promotions for organizing the release day event; Amber at Amber's Reading Room for her enthusiasm and offering to pimp out my books; and Rebecca Berto for reading the beginning chapters in early draft form and offering her comments and advice. You guys rock!

About the Author

Gemma James is a USA Today bestselling author of a blend of genres, from new adult contemporary to dark romance. She loves to explore the darker side of human nature in her fiction, and she's morbidly curious about anything dark and edgy, from deviant sex to serial killers. Readers have described her stories as being "not for the faint of heart."

She warns you to heed their words! Her playground isn't full of rainbows and kittens, though she likes both. She lives in middle-of-nowhere Oregon with her husband, two children, and a gaggle of animals.

For more information on available titles, please visit www.authorgemmajames.com

Made in the USA
Las Vegas, NV
21 December 2023

83303379R00111